Y0-BGE-888

DATE DUE

TAKING A STAND AGAINST
HUMAN RIGHTS ABUSES

TAKING A STAND
AGAINST
HUMAN RIGHTS
ABUSES

BY MICHAEL KRONENWETTER

Franklin Watts 1990
New York London Toronto Sydney

Photographs courtesy of: AP/Wide World: pp. 12, 45, 108; Magnum
Photos: pp. 15 (Jean Paul Paireault), 58 (Bruno Barbey), 65 (Chris
Steele-Perkins), 74 (Paul Fusco), 81 (St. Perkins); The Bettmann
Archive: p. 27; The Granger Collection: pp. 32, 35; Gamma Liaison:
p. 48 (Jacob Sutton); UPI/Bettman Newsphotos: pp. 61, 62, 82, 90;
Photo Researchers: p. 94 (David M. Grossman).

Library of Congress Cataloging-in-Publication Data

Kronenwetter, Michael.
Taking a stand against human rights abuses/Michael Kronenwetter
p. cm.
Includes bibliographical references.
Summary: Discusses governments that abuse human rights and
suggests what one can do to voice opposition to these oppressive regimes.
ISBN 0-531-10921-6
1. Civil rights—Juvenile literature. 2. Human rights—Juvenile
literature. [1. Human rights.] I. Title.
JC571.K725 1990
323—dc20   89-70450 CIP   AC

CONTENTS

TAKING A STAND AGAINST
HUMAN RIGHTS ABUSES

ONE

WHY SHOULD YOU CARE ABOUT HUMAN RIGHTS?

The people described below were unknown to each other. They were of different ages. They came from different countries and different social backgrounds. Some were poor. Others were middle class. Some were prominent citizens in their communities. Others were unknown. Some had left-wing political beliefs. Others had right-wing political beliefs. Some had no political beliefs at all.

But, as different as they were, they all had one thing in common. They were all victims of human rights abuses. Unfortunately, they are far from alone.

Stephen Biko, South Africa

Stephen Biko was thirty years old when the South African State Security Police arrested him in September 1977. The young black man was one of the most popular leaders of the opposition to the South African government's policies of racial separation known as apartheid. The Security Police, who were white, hated Biko because of his political activities.

They took Biko to jail and held him there for nineteen days. The details of what went on during those nineteen days are unknown, but it is clear that for much of the time he was kept naked to humiliate him and chained to keep him helpless. It is also clear that he was brutally tortured. They beat him mercilessly until he was nearly dead.

Even then, the police did not call for doctors to treat him, or take him to a nearby hospital. Instead they loaded his broken body into the back of a Land Rover and set out for a prison hospital seven hundred miles away. Either on the way or soon after reaching the distant hospital, Biko died.[1]

Ines Angelica Diaz Tapia, Chile

Ines was sitting in a cafe in the capital city of Santiago when a crowd of men burst into the room. They grabbed her and dragged her out the door. They shoved her into a waiting car and quickly sped away with her.

A few days later she was brought before a military court. Although she had been a healthy twenty-five-year-old woman when last seen in public, she was now so weak from exhaustion and physical abuse that she could hardly stand. For the four

Steve Biko, a leading opponent of South Africa's policy of apartheid, was tortured and beaten to death by government security police in 1977.

days since she'd been taken from the cafe, she had been beaten, burned with cigarettes, and subjected to electric shocks. Whenever she had passed out, her captors had revived her to make sure she suffered every moment of the pain they were inflicting on her.

Seeing a family member in the courtroom, she tried to speak to her. A guard immediately silenced her with a blow and took her away again. Perhaps because of this incident, her eventual trial—for a "crime" that has not been described—was held in secret.[2]

Leonid Plyushch, Union of Soviet Socialist Republics

Government psychiatrists decided in 1972 that Leonid Plyushch was mentally ill. They decided he had to be unbalanced because he'd helped start an organization that protested human rights abuse in the Soviet Union. Since the Soviet government insisted it never violated anyone's human rights, Plyushch's claim that it did proved that he was unstable.

While Plyushch was in the "hospital," the psychiatrists turned their diagnosis into reality by injecting him with mind-destroying drugs. By his own testimony, they transformed the once healthy and independent young man into a physical and emotional invalid. Eventually the drugs made him so helpless that he could not even leave his bed.[3]

Soh Joon Shik, Republic of South Korea

Soh was sentenced to seven years in prison for political crimes against the government of South Ko-

Soviet dissident Leonid Plyushch with his wife in Paris soon after they were allowed to emigrate. Plyushch had been confined to a mental institution for two and a half years because of his activities on behalf of human rights.

rea's dictatorial President Park Chung Hee in 1971. But when his sentence was up in 1978, Soh was not released. He was merely taken from the ordinary prison in which he had been held and thrown into a special kind of prison in the city of Kwangju.

The Kwangju prison was—and still is—a "protective custody center." The people held there are not ordinary prisoners. They have not been convicted of specific criminal acts. In fact, most of them are not even accused of committing specific crimes. Like Soh, they are only "suspected" of "intending to break the law."

In 1979, the year after Soh was thrown into Kwangju, President Park Chung Hee was assassinated. In 1981 South Korea proclaimed a new constitution. Since that time, therefore, the government that threw Soh into Kwangju prison has no longer existed. Yet Soh is still there. There is no way for him or his family to know when—if ever—he will get out.[4]

Safia Hashi Madar, Somalia

Safia was not particularly active in political affairs. She did, however, have a relative who was a political prisoner in their native Somalia. Safia herself may have even participated in a demonstration calling attention to her relative's plight. In any case, the Somali government was angered by that demonstration. It arrested Safia and threw her into prison.

The authorities apparently didn't care that the thirty-one-year-old woman was pregnant. (Her baby was born just three days after her arrest.) Soon afterward the new mother was tortured. After ten months of imprisonment and brutal treatment, she was sentenced to life in prison.[5]

Guillermo Florenciagni, Paraguay

Little Guillermo was only thirteen years old when he was arrested, just five days before Christmas 1986, in his hometown in Paraguay. He was suspected of stealing a bicycle. For this offense, the police held him in jail without a trial for a whole month. While he was there, they tortured him, presumably to force a confession.

When the authorities finally released him, he was terribly sick. His health had been destroyed by his imprisonment. His spleen was horribly swollen, and he had bruises all over his body, even on the soles of his feet. They were the kind of bruises you get only from torture. He was taken to a hospital, but it was too late. He died there on January 23.[6]

Yves Volel, Haiti

Yves Volel was a prominent attorney in Haiti in 1987. Opposed to the small group of military and civilian leaders then in power in the country, he looked forward to the day when the junta would be replaced by an elected government. He himself was running as a candidate for president of the country in the first election that was to be held under Haiti's new constitution.

In the meantime he remained active as a lawyer. One of his clients was a prisoner named Jean Raymond Louis. Yves had word that Louis, who was held illegally, was being tortured in jail. On October 13, 1987, Yves was talking to a group of reporters about the case, outside a public building in Haiti's biggest city, Port-au-Prince. He had a copy of Haiti's constitution with him as he pleaded his client's case to the press. While he was talking, plainclothes police came up and shot him to death in the street. He died with his copy of the Haitian constitution still clutched in his hand.[7]

WHAT ARE HUMAN RIGHTS?

Human rights are the most fundamental of all rights. In the simplest terms, they are the rights to life, liberty, and a decent human existence. In broader terms, they include all the political, social, and economic rights necessary for people to live dignified lives.

A United Nations publication describes them as those rights and freedoms that

> *allow us to fully develop and use our human qualities, our intelligence, our talents and our conscience and to satisfy our spiritual and other needs. They are based on mankind's increasing demand for a life in which the inherent dignity and worth of each human being will receive respect and protection.*[8]

The essential element of all human rights is that they belong to everyone. They are, in the words of the U.N. Universal Declaration of Human Rights, "the equal and unalienable rights of all members of the human family."

It doesn't matter how wealthy people are, how poor they are, what color they are, what country they come from, what political party they support, or what religion they believe in. They all—*we* all—

share the same human rights as everyone else. And since they belong to all of us, we all have an interest in protecting them.

WHY SHOULD YOU CARE ABOUT HUMAN RIGHTS?

Some of you might wonder why you should care about human rights abuses in places like the Soviet Union, Haiti, and Somalia. "It's too bad people's rights are being violated," you might be thinking, "but why should *I* care? No one is abusing *my* human rights. No one is throwing me into jail for my political beliefs. I can go to church any time I want. If I'm old enough, I can vote. I can write or say anything I want, and no one is going to torture me or kill me because of it."

In fact, there are many reasons for you to care about human rights abuses. One, of course, is simple human compassion—the sympathy we feel for our fellow human beings who are suffering. It is hard to think about people like Soh Joon Shik, Safia Hashi Madar, and the rest without wanting to help them.

But concern for others is not the only reason to care. Self-interest is involved as well. Whenever anyone's rights are violated, everyone's rights are put in danger. History shows that human rights abuses have a way of spreading. The same government that violates someone else's rights today can violate yours tomorrow. This was shown most dramatically—and most horribly—in Nazi Germany in the years before World War II. The Nazi government began by persecuting certain unpopular political and ethnic minorities, like the Communists and the Jews. When they got away with doing that, they began to persecute any and all groups who opposed them—and even some who didn't.

The terrible effects of human rights abuses do not stop at national boundaries. In many areas of the world today, refugees running away from tyrannical governments are flooding across their countries' borders and into neighboring lands. Some of them are fleeing political persecution. Others are fleeing economic and social conditions so terrible as to amount to a denial of their right to human dignity. But each of these desperate men, women, and children need food, shelter, medical care, and some way to make a living. Their demands put heavy strains on the countries to which they flee.

As James A. Banks, President of the National Council for the Social Studies, has pointed out, even the United States has suffered from these kinds of strains. "When Haitian and Cuban refugees fled from their nations to the United States, they had a significant impact on the Miami area and exacerbated ethnic conflict. The Mexicans who cross the Rio Grande seeking jobs in the United States affect jobs and educational opportunities for Americans, especially Mexican Americans."[9] If the human rights situations in Mexico, Haiti, and Cuba were improved, it would greatly relieve the pressures near our country's borders.

Perhaps most dramatically of all, human rights abuses often lead to revolution and war. One almost inevitable effect of such abuses is social unrest. At times, this unrest leads to outright rebellion. Most, if not all, of the revolutions that have transformed the world in the past few centuries were caused—at least in part—by violations of human rights.

Human rights abuses can even threaten the peace of the entire world. The same Nazi government that persecuted people within Germany soon began swallowing up neighboring countries and abusing the rights of their citizens as well. Before long, the nations of the world were thrown into the holocaust of World War II.

The danger human rights abuses pose to world peace led the General Assembly of the United Nations to pass the Universal Declaration of Human Rights on December 10, 1948. This historic document proclaimed human rights to be "the foundation of freedom, justice and peace in the world."[10] The U.N. recognized that when that foundation crumbles anywhere, freedom, justice, and peace are thrown into danger everywhere.

A teenager named Anne O'Brien, who is active in human rights work in her high school, put it another way. "The way I see it," she said, "in order to get along in this world, you need happiness not just for yourself, but for other people too."[11]

Americans have a special reason—and duty—to care about human rights. The United States has been a symbol of human rights ever since it was founded. As the poet Archibald MacLeish has put it: "There are those who will say that the liberation of humanity, the freedom of man and mind are nothing but a dream. They are right. It is a dream. It is the American dream."[12]

It is because of this basic "American dream" that former President Ronald Reagan once described human rights as "a cause that goes to the heart of our national character and defines our national purpose."[13] And President Jimmy Carter proclaimed, "[It is] imperative that we, as Americans, stand firm in our insistence that the values embodied in the Bill of Rights, and contained in the Universal Declaration [of Human Rights] be enjoyed by all."[14]

YOU CAN HELP

Perhaps the most important reason for you to take a stand against human rights abuses is a private one: the sense of personal worth, and empowerment, you will get from standing up for something important—something you believe in. "It is," as one high school student told me, "a small way we can have a say in what's going on in the world."

It is really not a small way at all. By working for human rights you can make a real and important difference in "what's going on in the world." You can help make it a better place for all of us to live in.

There are uncounted thousands of people whose rights are being abused right now. Many of them are being oppressed, tortured, and even murdered, as you read these words. You can help end their suffering.

There are, as we will see, many ways for you to act. This book can help you to teach the people around you to understand the reality of human rights abuse. It will help you to reach politicians and other leaders, and to encourage them to join the fight against human rights abuses. You can even play a direct part in freeing political prisoners: real human beings who are, at this very moment, suffering cruel and degrading conditions in prisons around the world.

But before you can work effectively to end human rights abuses, you have to understand what human rights are and why they are important. You have to find out where they are being abused, who is abusing them, and why. Then you have to learn what you can do to stop the abuses.

TWO

DEFINING HUMAN RIGHTS: THE GREAT DOCUMENTS

Where do human rights come from?

The answer, according to many philosophers, is that they don't "come from" anywhere. They are "natural" rights. The U.N.'s International Covenant on Economic, Social, and Cultural Rights says that they "derive from the inherent dignity of the human person."[1] As the French philosopher, Jacques Maritain, has written: "The human person possesses rights because of the very fact that it is a person, a whole, a master of itself and its acts."[2]

Most Christian, Jewish, and Islamic thinkers (along with believers in other religions) go one step further. Because they believe that human nature comes from God, they argue that human rights are God-given, too. It was this belief that Thomas Jefferson expressed in the Declaration of Independence when he wrote that "all men . . . are endowed by their Creator with certain unalienable rights."

But, although human rights are ours by nature, they need to be fought for and protected by law and tradition. In this chapter we will discuss some of the historic documents that have helped to lay the foundation for this.

PRE-ENLIGHTENMENT IDEAS OF HUMAN RIGHTS

The idea that all human beings share certain fundamental rights—just because they *are* human beings—is an old one. So is the idea that the biggest threat to those rights comes from the power of governments.

Father Robert F. Drinan, the Catholic priest and former U.S. Congressperson, has pointed out that "The desire to protect the individual from the abuse of power by a monarch, a tyrant or the state has its roots in the traditions and faiths of India, China, Japan, Persia (modern Iran), Russia and other nations."[3]

Even some monarchs themselves recognized the need to treat their subjects fairly. Four thousand years ago, an Egyptian ruler had this proud boast engraved on his coffin: "I have made every man equal to his fellow."[4] And the very first legal code that has come down to us—proclaimed almost four thousand years ago by the Babylonian ruler, Hammurabi—was established "to cause righteousness to appear in the land . . . that the strong harm not the weak."[5]

The third-century Chinese philosopher, Hsun-tzu, argued in favor of the rights of individuals. "What makes society possible?" he wrote. "Individual rights. What makes individual rights tenable? Justice. Therefore when justice and rights are adjusted, there is harmony. Where there is harmony, there is unity."[6] In other words, if a society is to be peaceful and unified, its rulers have to respect the individuals within it.

Virtually every major religion has taught the brotherhood and the dignity of all human beings. Mohammed, the founder of the Islamic religion, proclaimed that "All men are equal, like the teeth of a comb."[7] And the essence of human rights is summed up in the Jewish Talmud's instruction: "Do not do to your neighbor what you yourself would not like; that is the whole of the law, and all the rest is but commentaries."[8]

But the fact that philosophers and religious leaders believed in certain basic human rights does not mean they had the same idea of what those rights were that we have today. Few believed that women had the same rights as men, for example. Many accepted the institution of slavery, and some even owned slaves themselves.

THE AGE OF ENLIGHTENMENT

Our modern ideal of human rights began to take shape only during the so-called Age of Enlightenment of the seventeenth and eighteenth centuries.

Seventeenth-century English philosopher John Locke. His belief in the rights to life, liberty, and property helped inspire the American and French revolutions.

26

At that time certain liberal European philosophers began to change the ways people looked at the world and at themselves. The most influential was an Englishman named John Locke (1632–1704). It was Locke who laid down the three great cornerstones of the western ideal of human rights: the rights to life, liberty, and property.[9]

THE DECLARATION OF INDEPENDENCE AND CONSTITUTION OF THE UNITED STATES

The ideas of Locke and the other Enlightenment thinkers helped form a basis for the American and French Revolutions of the eighteenth century. Those two revolutions, in turn, resulted in some of the basic documents that help to define the modern ideal of human rights.

At least two of the most important American revolutionaries—Thomas Jefferson and Benjamin Franklin—are considered Enlightenment thinkers themselves. When Jefferson set out the reasons for the Revolution in the Declaration of Independence, human rights were at the head of his list. "We hold these truths to be self-evident," he wrote, "that all men are created equal, that they are endowed by their Creator with certain unalienable Rights, that among these are Life, Liberty, and the Pursuit of Happiness." These were almost exactly the rights that Locke had named (the right to "property" was replaced by the more general right to "the Pursuit of Happiness").

The Declaration went on to maintain that "Governments are instituted among men" precisely "to secure these Rights." And that "whenever any Form of Government becomes destructive of these ends, it is the Right of the People to alter or to abolish it."

Eleven years later the leaders of the new nation drew up the United States Constitution. That document remains today the fundamental law of the land. The Constitution was not primarily intended as a human rights document. It was an attempt to design a government that worked. But the design was made by people who were determined to protect the people's rights against that very government.

This fact was made clear in the Constitution's first sentence. It announced that the new government was being formed to "establish justice" and to "secure the blessings of liberty to ourselves and our Posterity." In other words the purpose of the new government would be the same purpose Jefferson had proclaimed in the Declaration of Independence—to secure the rights of the American people. But what exactly were these rights?

Life, liberty, justice, and *happiness* are stirring words, but they are not defined. If people have a right to life, does that mean there must be no death penalty? Does the right to liberty mean that people can do whatever they want, regardless of the consequences? Does it mean that all the jails have to be closed, because putting people in jail takes away their liberty? What is justice? And does a person's right to pursue happiness mean that he or she can make those around them *un*happy?

It was clear to some people that, if these rights were to be protected, they would have to be spelled out in more detail than either the Declaration of

Independence or the Constitution had done thus far. This process was begun by the first ten amendments to the Constitution, passed in 1791. Known as the Bill of Rights, they spell out certain basic rights and forbid the government to violate them. They were based, in part, on similar laws already adopted by various state legislatures.

The First Amendment proclaimed the rights to freedom of the press, speech, and religion. It also established two key political rights, the rights of people "peaceably to assemble, and to petition the Government for a redress of grievances." In other words, the First Amendment established the right to protest.

The nine amendments that followed proclaimed the right of U.S. citizens "to be secure in their persons, houses, papers, and effects, against unreasonable searches and seizures"; to be assured "due process of law"; to receive a "speedy and public trial by an impartial jury" when accused of crimes; and to be free from all threat of "cruel and unusual punishments"—along with several other rights.

Ironically, one reason that these rights had not been put into the Constitution in the first place was the desire to protect them. Some delegates to the Constitutional Convention were afraid that naming some rights would imply that they were the only rights the people had. Their fears were eventually overcome by the Ninth Amendment, which states that "The enumeration in the Constitution of certain rights shall not be construed to deny or disparage others retained by the people."

Later human rights amendments have outlawed slavery and other forms of "involuntary servitude" (the Thirteenth); assured black people (the Fifteenth), women (the Nineteenth), and eighteen-year-olds (the Twenty-sixth) the right to vote; and forbidden states to limit the right to vote by placing special taxes on voters (the Twenty-fourth).

The Constitution has never been completely effective as a protection of Americans' human rights. Even as the Bill of Rights was being written, slavery was practiced over much of the new country—and even by some of the same men who were writing it! Over the next century, the rights of the Native Americans would be trampled on again and again.

Several times in our history the rights of freedom of speech and of the press have been taken away from political dissidents (that is, people opposed to the government).[10] And during World War II, hundreds of thousands of Americans were sent to concentration camps, without trial, for the crime of having ancestors who came from Japan.

"THE RIGHTS OF MAN"

On August 26, 1789, in the midst of the French Revolution, the National Assembly of France proclaimed another great document in the history of human rights. Like the Bill of Rights, the "Declaration of the Rights of Man and Citizen" spelled out many of the most fundamental human rights.

"[C]onsidering that ignorance, forgetfulness, or contempt of the rights of man are the sole causes of public misfortunes," it proclaimed: "Men are born and remain free and equal in rights."

The general rights named in the Declaration were similar to those named by Jefferson and

DÉCLARATION

DES DROITS DE L'HOMME

ET DU CITOYEN,

Décrétés par l'Assemblée Nationale dans les Séances des 20, 21, 23, 24 et 26 août 1789, acceptés par le Roi.

PRÉAMBULE.

Les représentans du peuple François, constitués en assemblée nationale, considérant que l'ignorance, l'oubli ou le mépris des droits de l'homme sont les seules causes des malheurs publics et de la corruption des gouvernemens, ont résolu d'exposer, dans une déclaration solemnelle, les droits naturels, inaliénables et sacrés de l'homme ; afin que cette déclaration, constamment présente à tous les membres du corps social, leur rappelle sans cesse leurs droits et leurs devoirs ; afin que les actes du pouvoir législatif et ceux du pouvoir exécutif, pouvant être à chaque instant comparés avec le but de toute institution politique, en soient plus respectés ; afin que les réclamations des citoyens, fondées désormais sur des principes simples et incontestables, tournent toujours au maintien de la constitution et du bonheur de tous.

En conséquence, l'assemblée nationale reconnoît et déclare, en présence et sous les auspices de l'Être suprême, les droits suivans de l'homme et du citoyen.

ARTICLE PREMIER.

LES hommes naissent et demeurent libres et égaux en droits; les distinctions sociales ne peuvent être fondées que sur l'utilité commune.

ART. II.

LE but de toute association politique est la conservation des droits naturels et imprescriptibles de l'homme; ces droits sont la liberté, la propriété, la sûreté, et la résistance à l'oppression.

ART. III.

LE principe de toute souveraineté réside essentiellement dans la nation; nul corps, nul individu ne peut exercer d'autorité qui n'en émane expressément.

ART. IV.

LA liberté consiste à pouvoir faire tout ce qui ne nuit pas à autrui. Ainsi, l'exercice des droits naturels de chaque homme, n'a de bornes que celles qui assurent aux autres membres de la société la jouissance de ces mêmes droits; ces bornes ne peuvent être déterminées que par la loi.

ART. V.

LA loi n'a le droit de défendre que les actions nuisibles à la société. Tout ce qui n'est pas défendu par la loi ne peut être empêché, et nul ne peut être contraint à faire ce qu'elle n'ordonne pas.

ART. VI.

LA loi est l'expression de la volonté générale; tous les citoyens ont droit de concourir personnellement, ou par leurs représentans, à sa formation; elle doit être la même pour tous, soit qu'elle protege, soit qu'elle punisse. Tous les citoyens étant égaux à ses yeux, sont également, admissibles à toutes dignités, places et emplois publics, selon leur capacité et sans autres distinctions que celles de leurs vertus et de leurs talens.

ART. VII.

NUL homme ne peut être accusé, arrêté, ni détenu que dans les cas déterminés par la loi, et selon les formes qu'elle a prescrites. Ceux qui sollicitent, expédient, exécutent ou font exécuter des ordres arbitraires, doivent être punis; mais tout citoyen appelé ou saisi en vertu de la loi, doit obéir à l'instant; il se rend coupable par la résistance.

ART. VIII.

LA loi ne doit établir que des peines strictement et évidemment nécessaires, et nul ne peut être puni qu'en vertu d'une loi établie et promulguée antérieurement au délit, et légalement appliquée.

ART. IX.

TOUT homme étant présumé innocent jusqu'à ce qu'il ait été déclaré coupable, s'il est jugé indispensable de l'arrêter, toute rigueur qui ne seroit pas nécessaire pour s'assurer de sa personne doit être sévèrement réprimée par la loi.

ART. X.

NUL ne doit être inquiété pour ses opinions, mêmes religieuses, pourvu que leur manifestation ne trouble pas l'ordre public établi par la loi.

ART. XI.

LA libre communication des pensées et des opinions est un des droits les plus précieux de l'homme : tout citoyen peut donc parler, écrire, imprimer librement : sauf à répondre de l'abus de cette liberté dans les cas déterminés par la loi.

ART. XII.

LA garantie des droits de l'homme et du citoyen nécessite une force publique : cette force est donc instituée pour l'avantage de tous, et non pour l'utilité particulière de ceux à qui elle est confiée.

ART. XIII.

POUR l'entretien de la force publique, et pour les dépenses d'administration, une contribution commune est indispensable : elle doit être également répartie entre tous les citoyens, en raison de leurs facultés.

ART. XIV.

LES citoyens ont le droit de constater par eux-mêmes ou par leurs représentans, la nécessité de la contribution publique, de la consentir librement, d'en suivre l'emploi, et d'en déterminer la quotité, l'assiette, le recouvrement et la durée.

ART. XV.

LA société a le droit de demander compte à tout agent public de son administration.

ART. XVI.

TOUTE société, dans laquelle la garantie des droits n'est pas assurée, ni la séparation des pouvoirs déterminée, n'a point de constitution.

ART. XVII.

LES propriétés étant un droit inviolable et sacré, nul ne peut en être privé, si ce n'est lorsque la nécessité publique, légalement constatée, l'exige évidemment, et sous la condition d'une juste et préalable indemnité.

Se vend à Paris, chez GOUJON, marchand de musique, grand'cour du Palais-royal où se trouve le Tableau de la Constitution faisant pendant à celui-ci.

Locke. They were: "liberty, property, security, and resistance to oppression."

The first right of liberty was defined as "the power to do whatever is not injurious to others." So, the Declaration continued, "the enjoyment of the natural rights of every man has for its limits only those that assure other members of society the enjoyment of those same rights; such limits may be determined only by law."

The right of property was "sacred and inviolable," and no property could be taken away "unless a legally established public necessity obviously requires it," and then only after a "just and previous" payment was made.

No one was to be bothered "because of his opinions, even religious," so long as he did not "disturb the public order established by law." What is more, "Free communication of ideas and opinions is one of the most precious of the rights of man. Consequently, every citizen may speak, write, and print freely," although he or she would have to take "responsibility for the abuse of such liberty in the cases determined by law."

The Declaration of the Rights of Man and Citizen, passed by the French National Assembly in August 1789 at the beginning of the French Revolution, is a landmark document in the struggle for universal human rights.

The law was vital. Both the citizen and the state were bound to abide by it. One of the most important rights in the entire Declaration was that of equal treatment under the law. People accused of crimes were to be "considered innocent until declared guilty"; and, even when guilty, they were to be protected from any penalties that were not "absolutely and obviously necessary."

THE UNIVERSAL DECLARATION
OF HUMAN RIGHTS

The ideas enshrined in the Declaration of Independence, the U.S. Constitution, and the Declaration of the Rights of Man and Citizen all shared a common basis in the Enlightenment. And these ideas have, in turn, formed the basis for the ideals of human rights shared throughout the Western world today. They have clearly stirred something deep in the human spirit.

In the two centuries since the American and French revolutions, revolutions in scores of other countries have proclaimed the same rights set out in these documents. The governments established by these revolutions have often failed to respect those rights. But the ideal remains. In fact the ideal has been expanded.

That expansion is demonstrated in the many United Nations declarations and treaties that deal with human rights. At last count, there were some fifty-one of these.[11] It was natural for the U.N. to take the lead in defining human rights. The U.N. was founded in the wake of World War II, which had seen some of the greatest atrocities in modern times. The Nazis had set out to commit genocide

*Eleanor Roosevelt holds a copy of the
Universal Declaration of Human Rights,
the most important human rights
document of the twentieth century
(see Appendix A for complete text).*

(the destruction of a whole racial, religious, or ethnic group) against the Jews, the gypsies, and other groups. The war itself had resulted in the deaths of millions of people and the destruction of liberty for many millions more. Not surprisingly, the nations of the world came out of the war searching desperately for ways to see that such massive abuses of human rights would never happen again.

In founding the U.N., they were "determined . . . to save succeeding generations from the scourge of war . . . and to reaffirm faith in fundamental human rights, in the dignity and worth of the human person, in the equal rights of men and women and of nations large and small. . . ."[12]

The U.N. began by outlawing genocide in the U.N. Convention on Prevention and Punishment of Genocide, which was passed on December 9, 1948.[13] The next day, December 10, 1948, the U.N. passed the most important human rights document of the twentieth century—The Universal Declaration of Human Rights.

The Universal Declaration is the most sweeping expression yet of the international vision of human rights. (For the entire text of this historic document, see Appendix A.) The current U.N. Secretary-General, Javier Perez de Cuellar, has described its passage as "a landmark in the evolution of global life and civilization. It was the first time that the international community as a whole accepted the protection and promotion of human rights as a permanent obligation."[14]

Like the great American and French documents before it, the Universal Declaration upholds the traditional civil and political rights of life, liberty, property, equal treatment under the law, and freedom of opinion and belief. It outlaws slavery and torture. It confirms the democratic ideal that "everyone has the right to take part in the government of his country, directly or through freely chosen representatives." It asserts the right of every person to have a country, and the right of anyone who is persecuted in their own country to receive asylum (that is, protection from persecution) in other countries.

In addition to these civil and political rights, the Declaration also deals with social, cultural, and economic rights the earlier documents never dealt with. It declares, for example, that every person has a right to marry and raise a family, to receive an education, to obtain an adequate standard of living, to work, to join a trade union if he or she desires, and to receive fair pay for their work. It even proclaims a "right to rest and leisure." These rights, however, are much less universally acknowledged than the political and civil rights. For that reason, this book will concentrate mostly on abuses of those traditionally accepted rights that most governments agree on, even while they continue to abuse them.

The Universal Declaration of Human Rights is not a law. It is not legally binding on any nation, not even those who signed it. It only sets out "a standard of achievement for all peoples and nations" to work toward. Unfortunately, although *all* member nations of the U.N. formally subscribe to it, most of them regularly violate at least some of the rights spelled out in it.

Still, for those people committed to human rights, the U.N. Declaration is more than an expression of unrealistic hopes. "It is not just a piece of paper," proclaims Jack Healy, of the human rights group, Amnesty International U.S.A. "It's a fighting instrument."[15]

OTHER MAJOR
HUMAN RIGHTS DOCUMENTS

In the decades since 1948, the U.N. has enacted many other conventions and declarations on human rights. Perhaps the most important were passed by the U.N. General Assembly in 1966. They are the International Covenant on Civil and Political Rights, and the International Covenant on Economic, Social, and Cultural Rights (and an Optional Protocol). Along with the Universal Declaration, these Covenants are sometimes referred to as the International Bill of Rights.

Covenants are more binding than a simple declaration because those who sign them formally agree to abide by their conditions. As of the end of 1987, ninety-two countries had signed the International Covenant on International Economic, Social, and Cultural Rights, and eighty-seven had signed the Covenant on Civil and Political Rights. Thirty-nine had signed its Optional Protocol.[16]

But those figures have a dark side. They mean that many of the same nations that have already agreed to the Universal Declaration have refused to join the covenants. The United States is among them. The U.S. has neither signed nor ratified the International Covenant on Economic, Social, and Cultural Rights. And, although President Jimmy Carter signed the International Covenant on Civil and Political Rights in 1976, the Senate has never ratified it.[17] (A President can negotiate and sign a treaty on behalf of the U.S., but it is not legally binding until it is ratified by the Senate.)

Some people scoff at the International Bill of Rights. They point to all the countries that have not signed the Covenants and to all those that have signed but continue to abuse their people's rights. These documents, they say, are just collections of high-sounding words. But others, like Father Robert Drinan, disagree. These documents, he argues, amount to a human rights revolution

> *that seeks to change something fundamental in the way nations have operated. . . . (I)n times past, the establishment of a set of rules or laws like the Code of Hammurabi . . . or the U.S. Bill of Rights has eventually had an enormous impact. Consequently, there are many reasons to think that the promulgation of the International Bill of Rights, while seemingly an act that could be perceived as naive and unrealistic, may be one of the most important events in world history.[18]*

THREE

WHY GOVERNMENTS
ABUSE HUMAN RIGHTS

Governments, or armed groups seeking to take over governments, have always been the worst abusers of human rights. As Ira Glasser, of the legal rights group the American Civil Liberties Union, has said, "The people who violate [these] rights are people who hold power."[1] Governments hold more power than any other institution in society, for they hold political, economic, and military power all at once.

But why would governments want to use their power to abuse human rights? Governments and the people who want to control them give many excuses. But all their reasons finally boil down to one—the desire to obtain or to keep power.

WHAT KINDS OF GOVERNMENTS
ABUSE HUMAN RIGHTS?

Governments of all kinds have been known to abuse human rights. Historically, the right-wing government of Nazi Germany abused the rights of its citizens as terribly as did the left-wing Communist government of Joseph Stalin's Soviet Union or Mao Zedong's China. Today the white minority government of South Africa abuses the rights of its citizens, and so do the black governments of Ethiopia and Uganda.

Even countries with democratically elected governments have abused human rights. In recent years democratic countries like Colombia and the Philippines have been some of the worst persecutors of human rights supporters.[2]

Even Western, traditionally freedom-protecting governments like the United States have been known to abuse human rights. Even more ironically, governments acting in the name of religion are often among the worst abusers. During the Middle Ages, for example, governments allied with the Roman Catholic church burned people with opposing religious beliefs at the stake. Later the Protestant government of England beheaded Sir Thomas More for holding to his Roman Catholic views. Today the government of Iran brutally tortures and executes people who oppose its fundamentalist brand of the Muslim religion.[3]

Every country in the United Nations has signed the Universal Declaration of Human Rights. Most have signed at least some of the covenants and other international agreements upholding human rights as well. And yet, despite all this lip service to human rights, they are being abused every day in many countries around the world.

ARGUING ABOUT DEFINITIONS

Governments often justify their abuse of human rights by arguing about definitions. Not everyone agrees on just what is a human right and what is not.

Most governments agree that it is wrong to jail people for their beliefs. They deny holding political prisoners. Yet almost every country in the world has people in its jails whose "crimes" involved some kind of political activity.

Some of these prisoners have committed violent criminal acts but have done so for political motives. They have carried out terrorist bombings, for example, or destroyed government property to protest what they believe is government injustice. Others have committed nonviolent, but still outlawed, political acts. They have taken part in illegal demonstrations, for instance, or joined an illegal strike.

Still other prisoners have committed no specific illegal act at all. They have been imprisoned simply because they spoke out against the government in power. Or, as in Soh Joon Sikh's case, because the government is worried that they *might* do something in the future.

Just which of these people should be considered political prisoners is a matter of definition. One government's political prisoner may be another's dangerous criminal. All governments believe they have a right to protect themselves from being overthrown. What is more, they have a duty to protect their citizens from violence. At what point do these rights and duties begin?

A government facing an armed Communist revolution is likely to consider anyone speaking out in favor of Communism a threat. Even without a revolution of any kind, the Communist Party was banned in the United States in the 1950s. The U.S.

government assumed that all Communists were agents of the Soviet Union and were secretly plotting to overthrow the American government.

Imagine that a country is suffering from a constant pattern of armed attacks and bombings by Communist revolutionaries. Innocent men, women, and children are being killed and maimed. Surely the government is justified in fighting back and in jailing any of the attackers it can find. But is it justified in putting all Communists in jail?

What about jailing someone who encourages others to take up arms against the government but who does not actually take up arms himself?

The same question can be asked from the point of view of a Communist government, faced with armed attacks from rebels who claim to be fighting for democracy. Is this government justified in jailing anyone who speaks out for free elections?

The human rights group Amnesty International makes a distinction between what it calls prisoners of conscience and other political prisoners, who have been arrested for violent criminal acts. It defines prisoners of conscience as people detained because of their "beliefs, color, sex, ethnic origin, language, or religion who have not used or advocated violence."[4]

Most prisoners of conscience have been jailed for acts Americans take for granted: taking part in an antigovernment demonstration, for instance; belonging to a trade union, or participating in a strike; belonging to the wrong political party; making a speech against a government policy; writing a book, editorial, or pamphlet critical of the government; handing out antigovernment literature; or even having a family member who is accused of any of these things. Still others are in jail for practicing a banned religion or even for belonging to the wrong racial or ethnic group. There are thousands of these prisoners of conscience in scores of countries around the world.

FREEDOMS VERSUS NEEDS

Sometimes governments do not deny what they are doing or even quibble over how it should be defined. Instead, they argue that a limited amount of human rights abuse is justified because something even more important is at stake.

Governments often argue that individual rights have to be sacrificed to the greater good of society as a whole. Most governments give preference to certain kinds of human rights at the expense of others. Most often, this choice between rights is seen as a clash between needs and freedoms—that is, as a conflict between the people's right to have certain needs fulfilled and their freedom to do things in their own way.

Marxist governments, for example, tend to consider fulfilling people's economic needs more important than allowing economic freedoms. This is particularly true in poor Marxist countries, where the shortage of resources can mean misery and death for the majority of the people.

Such governments believe that the only way to provide food and shelter for their people is to impose a Marxist economic system controlled by the government. Under strict Marxism all means of producing goods—the factories, farms, mines, and other natural resources—must be kept in government hands.

*Fidel Castro, Communist leader of Cuba.
Marxist governments often claim that
political and economic freedoms are
incompatible with state-sponsored programs
to provide basic necessities to the people.*

Especially when a country has few resources, Marxists believe that what goods there are should be distributed as equally as possible. Private businesses, in which some people make profits at the expense of others, result in an uneven distribution of goods. Therefore capitalism and the making of profit are forbidden. These governments argue that the right to property must be sacrificed in favor of the right to food, clothing, and shelter.

Often they argue that political freedoms must be sacrificed, too. Any political activity threatening the Marxists' hold on the government undermines their ability to control economic activity. Without such control, private greed would soon destroy the essential fairness of the system. Under a real democratic system, they argue, people might be "deceived" into booting the Marxist government out of power. Then the people's rights to food and shelter would no longer be protected. Therefore, these governments reason, any movement toward real democracy must be suppressed.

Governments in democratic and capitalist countries see things differently. In these (usually much wealthier) societies, it is relatively easy to provide food and shelter to most of the people. Perhaps because of this, the governments and individuals alike tend to be more concerned with personal freedoms than with economic needs.

They accuse the Marxists of abusing what they see as the most fundamental of all the human rights—the freedom to control their own political, economic, and social affairs.

In economic matters they are concerned that people be allowed to profit from their labors. Feeling confident that most people's basic needs will be met, they turn their attention to people's freedom to use their excess wealth as they see fit.

But, while capitalists accuse Marxists of sacrificing political liberty, Marxists accuse capitalists of sacrificing the needs of the poor to the greed of the wealthy. In Marxists' eyes, the urban slums and the hordes of homeless people wandering through the streets of many Western cities are proof of worse repression than the holding of one-party elections. Each sees the other as violating important human rights. It is possible that both are right.

SACRIFICING HUMAN RIGHTS TO FOREIGN POLICY

The United States government often speaks out strongly against human rights abuses in countries unfriendly to it (for example, Iran and, until recently, the Soviet Union). But it rarely holds its friends and allies to the same high standard. In fact, human rights supporters complain that the U.S. often tolerates abuses committed by governments friendly to the United States.

There are many Americans—including some who believe strongly in the importance of human rights at home—who feel that the government is right to do so. They believe that human rights should play little or no part in American foreign policy.

According to foreign affairs analyst Vita Bite, this opinion was shared by many officials of the Reagan administration. They believed, according to Bite, "that the United States should not concern itself with how a government treats its own people (unless such actions directly threaten this nation)

Chilean leader General Augusto Pinochet, whose regime has at times engaged in brutal acts of repression. The U.S. government sometimes tolerates human rights abuses by friendly governments.

but rather with that government's conduct toward the United States and U.S. international interests."[5]

This feeling is often echoed by conservatives like writer Irving Kristol. "In extreme situations," he once wrote, "discussion of human rights becomes a luxury, and the governing principle then becomes: the enemy of my enemy is my friend."[6] The "enemy" these people are usually talking about is international Communism, led by the Soviet Union. No matter how oppressive an enemy of Communism may be, we must be their friend.

Supporters of this view point to President Jimmy Carter's experience with Nicaragua to make their case. Unlike President Reagan, Carter made human rights a cornerstone of his foreign policy. High administration officials, including Carter himself, often publicly condemned human rights violations by foreign governments, including some friends of the United States. Encouraged by Carter, Congress threatened to cut off financial and military help to governments that continued to abuse human rights.

In 1979 the Carter administration put heavy pressure on Anastasio Somoza, the brutal dictator of Nicaragua, whose government was one of the worst abusers in Latin America. When the abuses continued, the U.S. broke all military ties to Somoza. Within months his government fell to revolutionaries known as the Sandinistas. The Carter administration offered cautious help to the new government until this government also began to restrict the freedoms of the Nicaraguan people.

In the view of Carter's critics, the Sandinistas were much worse than Somoza had been. Many of them were admitted Marxists, and they accepted aid from the Soviet Union. By being overly concerned about human rights, the critics argued, Carter had caused Nicaragua to fall to the Communists. It was a clear demonstration, they said, of why a commitment to human rights should never dominate American foreign policy.[7]

Human rights advocates are appalled by these arguments. If the United States does not stand for human rights in its struggle against international Communism, they ask, what does it stand for? And how can the United States stand for human rights at home and ignore them abroad?

In the case of Nicaragua, they argue, it was not the United States's commitment to human rights that led to Somoza's fall. Rather, it was Somoza's lack of commitment to them. In the words of one Carter administration official, Warren Christopher, "In Nicaragua . . . decades of corrupt, oppressive rule finally led virtually the entire country to demand change. We could not have stemmed that tide of change, even if we had wished to do so."[8]

What kind of government Nicaragua would ultimately have would be up to the Nicaraguans. The choice the U.S. had was whether to support a brutal, corrupt, and wildly unpopular dictator, or hope for greater human rights in a new, more democratic Nicaragua. The Carter administration stopped supporting Somoza. As Carter's Secretary of State, Cyrus Vance, said, "championing human rights is a national requirement for a country with our heritage."[9]

JUSTIFYING TORTURE

Amnesty International U.S.A. defines torture as "any severe physical or mental pain intentionally inflicted for punishment, intimidation, confessions, or information by or at the instigation of a public official."[10]

Torture is used as a tool of both interrogation and intimidation. In interrogation it is used to force reluctant people to talk: either to confess to what they have done themselves or to bear witness against others. Sometimes it is used to verify testimony already given. Some torturers believe that information given under torture is more reliable than information given freely.

But there is a deeper, underlying reason for torture. Those who use it want to break the will of the people who oppose them. Torture is a great intimidator, for most people fear the prolonged pain of torture even more than they fear death. Torture, therefore, can be effective not only against the person actually being tortured, but against other potential enemies as well.

For many totalitarian governments this is all the justification they need. If torture can help to keep them in power, they will use it. But defenders of torture can be found in democratic countries as well as in totalitarian states.

In 1971 the British government admitted that the British Army had used abusive techniques in the interrogation (or questioning) of suspected Irish Republican Army terrorists in Northern Ireland. These techniques included hooding prisoners so that they could not see; subjecting them to excruciatingly loud noises for long periods of time; and keeping them from falling asleep.

The government set up a three-member board, known as the Parker Committee, to study whether the Army should continue to use such unpleasant methods in Northern Ireland. The majority of the committee decided that it should. Only one of the three prominent and respected members argued that such methods were both illegal and uncivilized.[11]

Officially, at least, the British government overruled the Parker Committee. But in the years since, the British government has been charged with an increasing number of human rights abuses against suspected IRA members.

In general, advocates of torture in democratic countries say that limits should always be put on its use. Torture is only justifiable when the enemy is particularly dangerous, or the situation particularly urgent. Even the majority of the Parker Committee did not favor unlimited use of torture against IRA prisoners. They argued only that *some* forms of "ill treatment" were acceptable under *some* circumstances.

But human rights advocates like Dr. Amelia Augustus of Amnesty International say that this is self-deception. "A little torture," she says, "is like being a little bit pregnant. Once a government gives in to torture, its use is bound to increase."[12] Former U.S. Attorney General Ramsey Clark agrees. "The notion that there are evil or dangerous people and that torture can be limited to them is contrary to history, experience and human nature," he says. "Once [torture] is justified," he claims, "those who merely oppose or threaten the authorities will suffer it."[13]

He insists that there is only one moral attitude to take about torture. "Torture must be unthinkable. To debate seriously the necessity or desirability of torture is to expose an absence of human values. To justify it in the name of realism, practicality and survival encourages the deadly game. To call for torture in the defense of freedom mocks freedom. People so insensitive to the nature of freedom as to invoke torture in its defense have already lost their freedom."[14] Most human rights advocates would agree.

FOUR

HUMAN RIGHTS ABUSES IN THE WORLD TODAY

It is impossible to describe all the many human rights abuses in the world in a single chapter. Instead this brief survey will be just that—a representative sampling of human rights abuses in the world today.[1]

RELIGIOUS PERSECUTION

People are denied full religious freedom in many countries around the world. Some governments, like those in Albania and North Korea, frown on the practice of *any* religion. Albania has actually executed people for upholding their religious beliefs.

A few countries permit only one religion to be practiced in public. Saudi Arabia, for example, not only forbids public services of any religion except Islam; it even forbids the wearing of the Christian cross. Iran, whose government is dominated by an extreme branch of the Islamic faith, has executed both Jews and members of the Baha'i faith.

The governments mentioned above are examples of extreme religious repression. Others, who permit some freedom of religion, give preference to some religions over others. The laws of Pakistan, for example, favor the Islamic faith. Buddhism is favored in Sri Lanka.

Even some countries that allow religious freedom in general forbid the practice of certain religions. In Zambia the Jehovah's Witnesses are outlawed. In China traditional Chinese religions are tolerated, but "foreign" religions, like Christianity, are forbidden.

In a few countries, like Iraq and Morocco, people are free to practice any religion they choose but are forbidden to try to convert others to their beliefs.

Some governments, including most in Eastern Europe, permit religions only under state supervision and control. In Czechoslovakia, members of the clergy are paid by the government. In these countries members of the clergy live under constant threat of harassment by the state.

RESTRICTIONS ON MOVEMENT

People in some countries are unable to live in the town of their choice, or even to travel freely, whether within their own countries or abroad. Citizens of Mozambique and North Korea, for example, need government permission to move to a new community. In countries like the Soviet Union residents need permits just to take a trip to another part of the country.

Black South Africans (who make up almost three-fourths of the population) need special passes before they can work in most regions of their country, and others to travel within them. Since 1960 over 3.5 million black South Africans have been forced from their homes by the South African government. Although the government claims that it has now ended such "forced removals," the evidence suggests that it has not.[2]

Citizens of some countries, including the U.S.S.R. and other nations of the Eastern bloc, cannot emigrate (that is, move out of their native country) without government permission. This permission is routinely denied. The wall that separated the divided German city of Berlin was a dramatic symbol of these restrictions. Although surrounded by the Eastern bloc country of the German Democratic Republic (or East Germany), West Berlin is tied politically to the German Federal Republic (West Germany). In 1961 East Germany built the wall to cut East Berlin off from West Berlin. In 1989, the East German government finally lifted restrictions on travel between East and West Germany.

FORCED LABOR

Although slavery, as such, is no longer legal anywhere, other kinds of forced labor are all too common. Serfdom, in which peasants born on a landowner's property have to farm that land for their entire lives, was common during the Middle Ages. Forms of it are still found in some countries, including Morocco and Brazil.

Forced labor camps, where prisoners are made to work for the government, exist in many totalitarian states. (A totalitarian state is any country ruled by a single person or party.) Forced labor camps are particularly common in certain Communist countries in Asia and Africa, where political enemies of the government are held in virtual slavery.

Ironically, children are forced to work even in some countries that have no forced labor for adults. (Taiwan and Hong Kong are two examples.) Child labor can also be found in Italy and Spain, even though it is technically illegal there. And India, whose constitution forbids forcing children to work, has the highest proportion of children working in the world.[3]

SEX DISCRIMINATION

Women have a different social position from that of men in most countries of the world. However, in most countries the basic human rights of both are equally protected by the law. In some, women are given special protections because of their vital role as mothers.

A number of U.N. declarations and conventions have spoken out against discrimination against women. Despite them, women are denied basic rights in many countries of the world. For example, in certain Islamic nations they are even considered unequal by law.

Most countries do have laws promising equal rights to women. In many places, however, they are rarely enforced. Discrimination against women is usually based on old social, religious, or political traditions. Because of this, it tends to be worst in the less developed areas of the world, like Bangladesh, Indonesia, and some of the more remote regions of Latin America.

Some kinds of discrimination against women can be found almost everywhere. Women's groups in the United States and Canada complain that even there women are often denied certain kinds of jobs or get paid less if they do get them. In certain parts of one highly developed nation—Switzerland—women are even denied the right to vote in local elections.[4]

DISCRIMINATION AGAINST MINORITIES

In many societies rights are denied to certain people because of their race, religion, or ethnic background. Relatively small, poor, or politically powerless minorities are especially vulnerable to these abuses.

The Miskito Indians of Nicaragua, for example, have been forcibly removed from their traditional homes by the Sandinista government. Roman Catholics in Czechoslovakia are subjected to harassment by the Communist government if they dare to practice their religion openly. People found handing out Roman Catholic religious tracts are subject to arrest. The Jewish *refuseniks*, who feel equally harassed in the Soviet Union, are denied permission to leave the country. Local Palestinians have been beaten, jailed, or deported for protesting

Women in certain Islamic countries are denied many basic rights.

59

the Israeli military occupation of the West Bank and Gaza Strip areas of the Middle East.[5]

In India tensions between the Muslim minority and the Hindu-controlled government have resulted in many cases of violent oppression. In 1987, for example, provincial police forces of the Uttar Pradesh province raided a village in the province and took hundreds of Muslim civilians into custody. Many of the prisoners were loaded into trucks in the middle of the night, taken to an isolated place, and shot to death. Their bodies were simply dumped into a canal. The very next day another provincial force attacked a nearby village. Although the government later claimed that "only" fifteen men, women, and children were killed, unofficial witnesses reported that many times that number had died.[6] In Sri Lanka, more than 680 members of the Tamil minority have vanished in the past five years alone. Human rights groups suspect that they have been killed by Sri Lankan security forces.[7]

Direct violence is not the only way minority rights are abused, of course. Social, economic, and political discrimination against minorities is common almost everywhere. When that discrimination is encouraged by the government, it becomes a serious human rights problem.

APARTHEID—DISCRIMINATION AGAINST THE MAJORITY

It's not always minorities whose rights are abused. In South Africa, where 70 percent of the people are black, the white minority has denied the rights of the black majority.

Palestinians in the occupied
Gaza Strip protest alleged
Israeli human rights abuses.

The situation in South Africa is unusual. As Professor Ivo D. Duchacek of the City College of New York has pointed out, "[T]oday, most national constitutions prohibit discriminatory practices based on race, ethnic origin, religion and sex."[8] But in South Africa, a whole legal system, known as the apartheid system, is based on racial segregation. The U.N. has accused the apartheid system of "slavelike practices."

Black South Africans need special "passes" to work or to travel within the country. In the wealthiest country in Africa, the great majority of the people have to live in segregated slums. Their children receive poor educations. Their homes are subject to searches by the police and security forces, without shown cause or warning. Quotas limit the number of black people who can work at high-paying jobs in certain industries. Many people are virtually forced to work at relatively poor-paying jobs in the gold mines that provide the nation with much of its enormous wealth.

Scene in the black township of Soweto, South Africa. Blacks in South Africa are required to live separately from whites and cannot travel or work in certain parts of the country without special passes.

Grim statistics demonstrate the results of the apartheid system. While the average white South African lives to age seventy, the average black South African dies at fifty-three. While 15 white babies out of every 1,000 die before they are one year old, 200 out of every 1,000 black infants do.[9]

POLITICAL REPRESSION

The right to peacefully oppose the policies of one's own government is the most basic of all political rights. If people can't criticize their government, how can they change it? Yet peaceful political opposition is repressed—that is, limited or denied—by governments around the world.

Of the thirty-three Asian countries surveyed for Charles Humana's *World Human Rights Guide*, for example, only nine (including Australia and New Zealand) allow total freedom of "peaceful political opposition," while twenty-four do not. In Africa, only four of the countries surveyed allow freedom of opposition while twenty-three do not. Six of the Central American and Caribbean nations listed in the *Guide* are at least somewhat repressive. In all of Central America, only Costa Rica allows real political freedom. In South America the *Guide* lists five countries as politically free, compared to five that are not. Only in North America and Europe do more countries allow freedom of opposition than repress it.

The kind of political repression varies widely. Some countries ban specific political parties, others whole points of view. Malaysia, for example, bans all Marxist political activity. Indonesia, which allows political opposition in general, still cracks down on separatists campaigning for independence for certain Indonesian islands.

The degree of repression varies even more widely. In Singapore, for example, a political opponent of the government can be temporarily jailed as a "security risk." In Iraq even peaceful political activity can result in the death penalty.

In some countries political opposition is crushed without any legal process at all. Political opponents are simply beaten or killed by the police, the army, or unofficial "death squads." In several countries these murders have become almost commonplace. In one of many recent incidents in El Salvador, troops arrested five young men, tortured them, shot them, and threw their bodies down a well. A few months later a coordinator of the nongovernmental Human Rights Commission of El Salvador was gunned down by an unidentified death squad while getting his children ready for school.[10] And in Colombia, hundreds of members of left-wing political organizations have been killed in recent years. In 1987, according to Amnesty International, "scores of trade unionists, students, university professors and human rights activists" were killed by death squads in the city of Medellìn alone.[11] In both these countries death squads have been so bold that they've published in advance lists of the people they intended to kill.

POLITICAL PRISONERS AND PRISONERS OF CONSCIENCE

Governments that stifle political dissent usually throw political dissenters into prison. Many thousands of people now suffer in jail cells as a result of

"Death squad" victims in El Salvador.

their political beliefs or activities. Shockingly, fully half the countries in the world are holding prisoners of conscience today. Many more have prisoners charged with criminal offenses committed out of political motives. It is hard for these dissidents to receive fair trials in most countries of the world. In some cases, they receive no trial at all. As we have already seen in the case of Soh Joon Shik, some countries hold prisoners for years without trial, or long after their legally imposed sentences have been served.

In some countries the proportion of political prisoners is staggering. Nicaragua, a country with only 3,342,000 people, admitted to holding 3,434 political prisoners at the end of 1987.[12] Opponents of the Sandinista government claim that there are many more. In 1987 the Turkish Human Rights Association reported that there were 18,000 political prisoners in that country.[13] In Albania there are actually more political prisoners than ordinary criminals in the nation's jails![14]

Among Western European governments the United Kingdom (or Great Britain) is probably the worst offender. In its determination to end unrest in Northern Ireland, it has denied several traditional legal rights to suspected Irish terrorists. Among these are the right not to be imprisoned without specific criminal charges, and the right to remain silent without having that silence used against them in court. As of early 1989 the European Court of Human Rights had ruled against the United Kingdom in twelve separate cases—more than against any other Western European government.[15]

TORTURE

Torture is one of the most shameful of all forms of human rights abuse because it is deliberately intended to destroy the dignity of the victim. It is almost universally condemned by spiritual and political leaders alike. Yet torture is—and always has been—in widespread use around the world. According to Amnesty International, torture is still practiced "on a systematic basis" in nearly seventy different countries.[16]

Common types of physical torture include simple beatings as well as more sophisticated means of producing pain such as electric shocks, drugs, and acids. Psychological torture includes subjecting prisoners to harsh conditions such as extreme filth, total isolation from all human contact, constant heat or cold, the "sensory deprivation" of total darkness, or the "sensory overload" of unrelenting loud noise or constant bright lights. It also includes depriving people of sleep, food, clothing, or needed medical care, or humiliating them by keeping them naked or by abusing them sexually.

International agreements against torture include the OAS (Organization of American States) Inter-American Convention to Prevent and Punish Torture, which went into effect in February 1987, and the European Convention for the Prevention of Torture and Inhuman or Degrading Treatment or Punishment, passed by a committee of the Council of Europe in June of 1987.

Most important of all is the United Nations Convention against Torture and Other Cruel, Inhuman, or Degrading Treatment or Punishment, which went into force in June 1987. The U.N. convention claims international jurisdiction over accused torturers and requires governments to investigate evidence of alleged torture, and to assist people who were victims of it. In addition it calls on countries not to deport or return refugees to countries in which they are likely to be tortured. By the end of 1987, twenty-eight countries were full parties to the convention.[17] Some thirty-seven other nations had signed it, but had not yet ratified it. The United States was not among either group.[18]

Signing, in any case, is no guarantee that a government will not use torture. Many of the worst offenders are countries that *have* signed the convention. Among the sixty-seven governments Amnesty International names as either practicing or tolerating torture "on a systematic basis" are Afghanistan, Bolivia, Brazil, Chile, China, Colombia, Egypt, Indonesia, Israel, Mexico, Morocco, the Philippines, Spain, Tunisia, Uganda, and the Union of Soviet Socialist Republics—all of whom have signed the convention.[19]

FIVE

PEOPLE
TAKING A STAND

What you have read so far may seem discouraging. If human rights are abused so badly and in so many different places around the world, what can be done to stop these abuses? How can ordinary people ever hope to affect the policies of torture, repression, and tyranny of so many governments? Is there any real reason to try? Or are those people who think they can do something about human rights abuses just kidding themselves?

Can individual people—whether acting alone or together—really do something about human rights abuses? Can they really make a difference? Can *you* really make a difference?

The answer is: Yes! Here we will meet a few of the many people around the world who already have made a difference. Some of them are world famous; others are almost unknown. But each of them has taken a stand against human rights abuses—and each has done something to end them.

FAMOUS LEADERS IN THE
STRUGGLE FOR HUMAN RIGHTS

Elizabeth Cady Stanton

For more than a century after the American Revolution, women were not able to vote in the United States. This denial of their most basic political right seemed right and normal to most Americans, male and female alike. But not to all. Among the exceptions was a woman named Elizabeth Cady Stanton.

Born in Johnstown, New York, in 1815, she was raised in a society that discriminated against all kinds of minorities. In the West the native American Indians were being driven from their lands and herded onto reservations. In half the states black people were regarded as property and not as human beings. And women everywhere were routinely denied many of the legal rights and protections given to men.

Elizabeth Cady Stanton rebelled against all forms of discrimination all her life. As a young woman she studied with her father, a judge, to become a lawyer—even though she could not legally practice law because only men were admitted to the bar.

She joined the campaign against slavery and married another abolitionist named Henry Stanton. But when the couple attended a big antislavery convention in London, England, she found that she and other women were forbidden to participate, because of their sex.

From that time on Elizabeth Cady Stanton threw herself wholeheartedly into the struggle for women's rights—and particularly for woman suffrage (the right of women to vote). With a few other concerned women she called the first Women's Rights Convention in history, at Seneca Falls, New York, in 1848. That historic convention passed a declaration calling for woman suffrage.

In 1869 she and Susan B. Anthony founded the National Woman Suffrage Association, which worked for an amendment to the U.S. Constitution giving women the right to vote. In 1890, when their group merged with the country's only other major woman suffrage group, Elizabeth was named as the new organization's first president.[1]

She and the other women who made up the woman suffrage movement—including Lucretia Mott, Lucy Stone, Angelina and Sarah Grimké—were held up to public ridicule by those who opposed their cause. But they persisted.

But Elizabeth Cady Stanton never got to exercise the right to vote. She died in 1902. Thanks to her efforts, and those of the other brave women who fought with her, however, succeeding generations of American women have been able to exercise that right. The Nineteenth Amendment to the Constitution, giving them the vote, was passed by the Congress in 1918 and ratified by the states in 1920.

Mohandas K. Gandhi

Perhaps the greatest twentieth-century human rights leader was Mohandas K. Gandhi, the spiritual and political leader who led India's struggle for freedom from Great Britain in the 1930s and '40s.

Gandhi began working for human rights far from home, fighting for the rights of Indians living in South Africa. Returning to his homeland, he campaigned not only against British rule, but also against the cruelties of India's own caste system.

Under this system one caste, or whole class of people, was treated almost as if they were a lower form of life. They were called Untouchables, because members of other castes avoided touching them, believing their touch would pollute them spiritually. Gandhi, on the other hand, referred to them as the "Children of God" and worked to improve their social position.

Gandhi sacrificed enormously for the cause of human rights. He was beaten and imprisoned many times. (His last term in a British prison came when he was in his seventies.) Even when he was free, he went on long and dangerous fasts to call attention to the far greater sufferings of the Indian people. His years of sacrifice were finally rewarded when India was granted its independence in 1948.[2]

Desmond Tutu

Archbishop Desmond Tutu is the most visible spokesperson for the black people of South Africa. As head of the Anglican Church in South Africa, he has an unusually well protected position for a black South African. It allows him to denounce apartheid publicly. He can also travel outside South Africa to encourage other countries to help pressure South Africa to abandon its racist policies.

Despite his privileged position, Tutu risks imprisonment, or worse, every time he speaks out against apartheid. Under South African laws other people have been tried and convicted of treason for saying and doing much less than he has done already.

The Archbishop's bravery and eloquence have

*Archbishop Desmond Tutu, head of
the Anglican Church in South Africa,
is a vocal opponent of the apartheid
system. In 1984 he was awarded
the Nobel Peace Prize.*

made him a central figure in the battle against apartheid. Within South Africa he has become a symbol of hope and determination. Outside, his persuasive powers have helped stir widespread international opposition to apartheid. This opposition, in turn, has put enormous pressure on the South African government.[3]

Lech Walesa

Lech Walesa of Poland, a symbol of the struggle for workers' rights around the world, is a leader of the independent trade union known as Solidarity. In Poland, as in most Communist countries, most industries are run by the government. Before Solidarity, workers in Poland were allowed to join only government-sponsored workers' organizations. These so-called unions did not really represent the interests of the workers at all. They represented the state. In conflicts between workers and government employers, they usually sided with the employers.

As a member of one of these organizations in 1976, Walesa insisted on bringing up the complaints of his fellow workers. He was fired from his job at a shipyard in Gdansk. He responded by organizing a real, independent union in Gdansk. Then, when the national Solidarity union was formed to fight for the rights of Polish workers, he was chosen as its chair.[4]

Solidarity soon became a rallying point for people opposed to the Polish government. The government reacted by outlawing the union. Walesa, however, continued to work on its behalf. Because of this, he suffered repeated harassment, intimidation, and even imprisonment. But he has become an inspiration to other workers around the world. In 1983, Walesa was awarded the Nobel Peace Prize. Now it appears that his long battle for Solidarity has succeeded at last. The Polish government has agreed to make Solidarity legal again, and in parliamentary elections in June 1989, Solidarity candidates won a landslide victory over Communist Party candidates.

LEADERS DO NOT ACT ALONE

All of these leaders have become symbols of the struggles they took part in. Of course none of them accomplished what they did alone. In each case their movements consisted of thousands of rank and file supporters.

For example, when the Nobel Prize committee awarded Archbishop Tutu the Nobel Peace Prize in 1984, it also honored, in the words of the Nobel committee, "the courage and heroism" of all those other "black South Africans in their use of peaceful methods in the struggle against apartheid."[6]

WORKING TOGETHER FOR HUMAN RIGHTS

Altogether, there are more than a thousand organizations working for human rights around the world, and their numbers are growing.

These local, regional, and national human rights groups include the Taiwan Association for Human Rights, the Turkish Human Rights Association, the Committee for the Defense of the Unjustly Persecuted (Czechoslovakia), the Philippine Alliance of Human Rights Advocates, the Cuban

Committee for Human Rights, and the Guyana Human Rights Association—to name just a few. In some countries there are separate, independent human rights commissions in almost every big city or district. Although many of these groups have official-sounding names, most have no connection with their governments. Instead, in many places, they are actively suppressed by the governments involved.

In addition to general human rights organizations, there are many others with specialized purposes. Some—like the Armenian Committee to Defend Political Prisoners (in the Soviet Union) and the Relatives of Detainees Disappeared in the Emergency Zone (in Peru)—were formed to help victims of specific abuses. Others were formed to carry out specific human rights activities. These include union groups that promote workers' rights and political reform movements that work for governmental changes.

In many countries they also include groups of lawyers who defend the rights of political prisoners and others whose rights are being abused. In the United States, for example, the American Civil Liberties Union often defends those whose constitutional rights are violated.

BLOWING THE WHISTLE ON HUMAN RIGHTS ABUSES

Governments and others who violate people's human rights do not stop their abuses of their own accord. When they stop, it is usually because of pressure. Sometimes that pressure comes from public opinion within the country involved. Sometimes it comes from outside. Sometimes it comes from other governments. Sometimes it comes from ordinary citizens.

Wherever the pressure comes from, it begins with information. Before either foreign governments or ordinary citizens can protest torture and murder, they have to know that it is going on, who is carrying it out, and who the victims are.

Repressive governments and other abusers rarely disseminate (or spread) that information themselves. It is up to other people—people who care about human rights—to collect and publish that information around the world.

Fortunately for the cause of human rights, there are brave people all around the world who make it their business to do just that. Risking harassment, violence, and even death, they do their best to tell the world about the abuses taking place within their countries, often by their own governments.

Some human rights monitors belong to organized human rights groups—like Americas Watch, which monitors the situation in Central and South America, or the Palestine Human Rights Information Center, which monitors abuses in Israel and the Israeli occupied territories. But some monitors act as individuals. Some are victims of human rights abuses themselves, or members of victims' families. Some are journalists whose job is to report what is happening. Some are labor leaders, educators, priests, ministers, and other religious workers, lawyers, members of relief and charitable groups, and other people who come across the victims of abuses in their work. Still others are simply private individuals who are outraged by abuses they see going on around them.

Unlike such famous human rights leaders as Walesa and Tutu, most human rights monitors are anonymous. Their names will never be known to the general public. But they are the heart and soul of the worldwide human rights movement.

Without them, human rights abuses would go unnoticed, except by the victims, even in the countries in which they occur. The information they collect in the most repressive countries is then publicized in freer countries by groups like Human Rights Watch in the United States and Amnesty International, which is based in England but has chapters in countries around the world. This publicity allows even the ordinary people in those countries—people like yourself—to bring international pressure to bear against the abusers.

But those who record and report intimidation, torture, and murder play another vital role as well. By letting others know about the pain and anguish of those whose rights are violated, they pay testimony to the essential dignity of the victims. In the words of Aryeh Neier, the executive director of Human Rights Watch, "One of the central functions served by human rights monitors is that, by recording abuses, they express respect for those who suffer."[7]

Monitoring human rights inside the United States involves few risks. Human rights groups have reported no serious cases of harassment against Americans for monitoring abuses inside the United States in recent years. In other countries, however, publicizing abuses can mean real danger. In some, human rights monitors risk suffering the same abuses as those they report happening to others.

Despite these risks, many brave people continue to gather and publicize information about human rights abuses. Even in countries like Colombia, Haiti, and the Philippines—where reporting abuses can mean torture and death at the hands of government security forces or unofficial death squads—they continue their heroic work.

According to Neier, "human rights monitoring is spreading. More and more citizens around the world are taking up the effort to gather information on the discrepancies between the practices of their governments and the commitments those governments have made" in signing documents like the U.N. Declaration of Human Rights.[9]

AMNESTY INTERNATIONAL

Of all the human rights groups in the world none makes better use of the information collected by human rights monitors than Amnesty International. With more than 700,000 members and volunteers in over 150 countries,[10] Amnesty is probably the world's largest human rights organization. It is also one of the most respected. According to the U.N. Secretary General, Javier Perez de Cuellar, it is also the most effective.[11]

Founded in 1961 to help people imprisoned because of their beliefs, Amnesty now has four major goals.

1. It works to free all "prisoners of conscience." In order to accept someone as a valid "prisoner of conscience," it asks only two things: that he or she has been imprisoned because of political or religious activities or beliefs; and did not commit, or advocate (urge), violence.

At Amnesty International headquarters in London, "urgent action" reports on victims of human rights abuses are prepared.

*Jacek Czaputowicz was imprisoned by the
Polish government for dissident activities.
Shown here soon after his release, he holds
two issues of the Amnesty International
newsletter translated into Polish.*

2. It tries to assure that all political prisoners, whether they are accused of violent acts or not, are given fair trials and decent treatment.
3. It works to end torture.
4. It seeks to ban capital punishment.

It seeks to accomplish these goals everywhere in the world. It is not concerned with any country's ideology. It does not concern itself with whether a government is democratic or totalitarian, Communist, or capitalist. It asks only that it respect human rights.

Every year Amnesty puts out a book-length report of abuses of human rights around the world. The most recent edition recorded abuses in 135 countries, from the United States to Burkina Faso in western Africa, and from the People's Republic of China to Grenada. It also publishes several more detailed studies of abuses in individual countries every year, as well as a stream of press releases on human rights crises as they occur.

But Amnesty is best known for the efforts of its members to free "prisoners of conscience" around the world. Working either individually or as members of more than 3,863 Amnesty chapters in forty-seven countries,[12] they pressure governments to release specific prisoners whose cases Amnesty has taken up. Day after day, week after week, and year after year, astonished government officials in scores of countries are flooded with their appeals.

The unending streams of letters and telegrams flow from and to all corners of the world. In the fall of 1988 the office of King Hassan of Morocco, in the royal palace at Rabat, was deluged with letters from people in many countries appealing for the release of an imprisoned socialist named Hassan El-Bou.[13] At the same time other palaces and embassies in capitals around the world were receiving similar letters about cases in their own countries. At any given moment, in fact, Amnesty works on behalf of some five thousand individual prisoners worldwide.[14]

The message that Amnesty's letters send to abusing governments is a simple one. *"We know what you are doing.* You may oppress your people. You may torture them. You may kill them. But if you do, you will not do it in secret. You will be held up to international shame and ridicule."

It may be a simple message, but it is also a tremendously powerful one. As Aryeh Neier has pointed out, governments "must pretend to respect human rights," whether they really do or not. That is why, as *Christian Century* Magazine has said, "even the most repressive regimes cannot simply ignore sustained international outcry against their inhumane policies. . . ."[15]

In a typical year, about one-third of the prisoners "adopted" by Amnesty International are freed. In 1987, the last year for which there are statistics, 1,689 of Amnesty's adopted prisoners were set free. Amnesty itself never claims the responsibility for any of these releases. "There are just too many elements in any decision [to free a prisoner] for us to claim credit," an Amnesty official has said.[16] But most observers—including many of the freed prisoners themselves—do give the group and its members a lot of the credit.

One grateful ex-prisoner of conscience from South Africa put it this way. "I know Amnesty International never takes credit for the release of prisoners, but if it was not for the many hundreds of letters sent to the South African Minister of Justice, I would not be here today."[17]

The hundreds of thousands of Amnesty letter writers around the world are inspiring examples of what people can do to fight human rights abuse. In 1977 Amnesty International was honored by a Nobel Peace Prize. In making the award, the Nobel Committee called Amnesty a "bulwark" in the defense "of human dignity against violence and subjugation."

SIX

THINGS YOU CAN DO
TO FIGHT HUMAN RIGHTS ABUSES

The people discussed in the previous chapter have accomplished a great deal. But the struggle for human rights is far from over. As we have seen, human rights have many enemies, and these enemies have enormous power. They have guns, tanks, prisons, and armies of soldiers, police, and torturers all over the world.

But fortunately, as Ira Glasser, the executive director of the American Civil Libertics Union, has said, "The outcome of these struggles never depends on the people who oppose liberty. It depends on the response—or the lack of response—of those who support it."[1] Those of us who support it must continue to respond, and to respond ever more strongly, and in greater and greater numbers. If we do, the enemies of liberty are bound to fail.

INFORM YOURSELF

If you want to join the ongoing battle against rights abuses, the first thing to do is to learn as much as you can about them. Reading this book is a good first step. Its bibliography lists several other books and articles that can help you expand your knowledge and understanding of human rights abuses.

But already published materials are not enough. It is important to keep up to date. The human rights situation in many countries is constantly changing. A sudden change in government, or a single new law, can bring about enormous changes in human rights almost overnight.

In the late 1970s and early 1980s, for example, Argentina had one of the worst human rights records in South America. Almost nine thousand political dissidents disappeared, most of them actually kidnapped and murdered by Argentina's cruel military government. The practice got to be so common that the Spanish word for "disappeared," *desaparecido*, began to take on new meanings in the language of human rights. *Desaparecido* became another word for murdered, and the victims themselves became tragically known as the *desaparecidos*.

When Argentina elected a new government in 1983, the disappearances stopped. The entire human rights situation in Argentina began to improve. Some of the military leaders responsible for the earlier atrocities were tried and found guilty in civilian courts. But only a few years later many of these encouraging human rights advances were threatened by a new law that protected many in the military from being tried for their crimes.[2]

Sudden and dramatic changes like these are happening all the time. But it is not hard to keep up. Major newspapers, and radio and television news programs, are filled with information about current human rights abuses. Organizations like Human Rights Watch and Amnesty International U.S.A. can give you constantly updated information on the current state of human rights abuses around the world (see Appendix E for addresses).

SPREAD THE WORD
ABOUT HUMAN RIGHTS

If educating yourself is the first step in doing something about human rights abuses, educating others is the second. In this busy world it is easy for most people to avoid thinking about human rights abuses. After all, most people are busy. They are going to school or working at a job or raising a family. They have very little time to give to matters that do not immediately concern them.

When they finally do have a spare moment, most people would rather spend it doing something more enjoyable than thinking about injustice, torture, and murder. Besides, most people in our society assume, human rights abuses happen to other people, in barbaric countries, far away. They don't have anything to do with *us*.

There are many ways to spread the word about human rights. The first—and for most people the easiest—is to talk about them. You can talk about human rights abuses with anyone you ordinarily talk to about other things—to your friends, to your parents, to your teachers. You can let them know the many ways rights are being abused, and where. Most importantly, you can help raise their consciousness about human rights, and why they are so important to everyone, everywhere.

You can find many natural opportunities to

discuss human rights abuses with people you know. At home, when you see a report of some violation of human rights on the TV news, you can discuss it with family members. The national elections that are held every two years provide wonderful opportunities to inform people about human rights. Find out where the candidates stand. Even if you're too young to vote yourself, ask your parents whom they plan to vote for, and discuss their candidates' stand on human rights issues with them.

At school, talk to your teachers about human rights. There are many activities you can do in or out of class that relate to human rights. A U.S. history class might make a timetable tracing the expansion of the right to vote from the time only white-adult-male-landowners could vote until today. A Spanish class might prepare a report on human rights abuses in the Spanish-speaking countries of Latin America. An art class could hold a contest to judge who makes the best design for a human rights poster.

You can ask both school and public librarians to be sure to get books dealing with human rights issues for their libraries. Many libraries have weekly or monthly exhibits that feature books on particular subjects. Suggest that they do exhibits on subjects related to human rights.

Even listening to rock music with friends can provide chances to discuss human rights. Many rock stars—from Bruce Springsteen to INXS and U2—have made statements supporting human rights. Some have done benefit concerts, or even tours, for Amnesty International. Several have songs that deal in powerful ways with human rights issues. Many of Tracy Chapman's lyrics are con-

*Singer Peter Gabriel during an
international tour organized by
Amnesty International. With him are
mothers of persons who disappeared in
Argentina and Chile during the
political repression of the seventies.*

cerned with questions of human dignity; Peter Gabriel's *Biko* deals with the murdered South African human rights leader; and Sting's *They Dance Alone* is a testament to the suffering of the mothers of Argentina's "disappeared"—to give just a few examples. Some of your friends may be unaware of what many of these songs are really about. You can share with them the real human tragedies behind the music. Listening to these singers with friends, or watching their videos on MTV or VH1, can be a springboard to a valuable discussion about human rights.

There are many other ways to raise the consciousness of your friends and other students about human rights. Ask your teachers if you can display human rights posters and other materials on the bulletin boards in their classrooms, for instance. If you have an artistic bent, it might be fun to design and make up your own posters or flyers. If not, some of the organizations listed in Appendix E may be able to supply you with brochures, newsletters, and other suitable materials to display or hand out at your school.

Talk to your principal. If she or he is sympathetic to your cause, you may be permitted to hang human rights materials in the halls, the cafeteria, or at other gathering places within the school. Some schools are even willing to devote a separate bulletin board to human rights materials on a regular basis. These materials not only raise the consciousness of the people who see them, they serve as spurs to conversation as well.

Some people see opportunities to talk about human rights everywhere. One high school student

I talked with picks a human rights theme whenever she is asked to choose her own subject for an assignment in school. If asked to give a book report, she might choose a book about Stephen Biko, or Dr. Martin Luther King, Jr., or some other hero of the human rights movement. If asked to give a talk-to-persuade in Speech class, she might try to convince her classmates that the U.S. should end foreign aid to governments that violate their own citizens' rights.

Another student I know won't drink Coke or any other soft drinks made by the Coca-Cola Company. When her friends ask her why she won't have a Coke, she tells them she is boycotting the company because it does business in South Africa. If all young Americans refused to drink Coke in protest, she tells them, the company would soon leave South Africa. This, in turn, would help pressure the government there to end its system of apartheid. Few if any of her classmates have joined her in her boycott. They are, she says jokingly, too "violently attached to their Coke machines." But all of them have learned more than they knew before about the cruelty of apartheid.

There are three things to keep in mind whenever you talk to people about human rights:

1. Be honest. Never make claims that you do not know to be true. The truth is on your side. Don't abuse it. As a practical matter, once someone catches you in a major misstatement, or even a drastic *over*statement, it's unlikely they will believe you in the future.

2. Be forceful, but be reasonable. Human rights is an intensely important issue. It is *good* to

feel strongly about it, and to let your feelings show. But at the same time you must not sound—or be—fanatic. If you come across as hysterical, people will not take you seriously.

3. Always be courteous. Listen to other people's points of view as respectfully as you want them to listen to yours. Remember, your goal is to inform them and to raise their consciousness about vital issues. It is not to intimidate them or to score points off them in an argument.

THE PEN REALLY CAN BE MIGHTIER THAN THE SWORD

Some people feel more comfortable writing about an issue than talking about it. If you are one of them, you can find many opportunities to write about human rights issues. Your school paper is a good place to start.

Talk to the editor about doing a feature on some burning human rights issue. It might be a hot subject in the news, or a more general statement of the importance of human rights. The yearly celebration of Human Rights Day, on December 10, the anniversary of the Universal Declaration, is a natural occasion for this kind of article. Offer to write the feature—or features—yourself.

Many school editors (and faculty advisers) are reluctant to publish articles on controversial subjects. They believe a school paper should not "take sides" on what might be considered a political issue. If this is the case in your school, point out to them that human rights is not really a political issue at all—it is a human issue. Every major political party

in the U.S. supports the principles of human rights, and every country in the entire U.N. has signed the Universal Declaration.

If they still won't accept your article, try a letter to the editor instead. Some editors (and advisors) will publish letters on subjects they wouldn't print articles about. They feel that a letter does not suggest that the paper, or the school, supports a particular position, the way that an article does. When writing this kind of letter, try to tie your subject to something going on in the school—even if it's only something that you have been learning about in a social studies class.

Because school papers are often shy about tackling controversial subjects, even in the Letters to the Editor column, you might have better luck writing to your local paper. Many smaller newspapers have open Letters to the Editor columns where they will print any letter from a reader, as long as it meets the paper's standards of good taste and its length requirements. Most other papers print at least some letters from readers, particularly if they respond to an article or editorial recently published in the paper. (Some magazines print letters as well.) Letters columns are widely read, and they make

Student journalism is an excellent vehicle for raising the consciousness of your peers about human rights abuses throughout the world.

excellent outlets for human rights information. Tips on writing letters to the editor appear in Appendix C.

WRITING TO
FOREIGN GOVERNMENTS

As we have seen, many governments that abuse their citizens' human rights like to believe they are acting in secret. They like to think that the world does not know what they are doing (or, if it does know, that it does not care). You can help break down this illusion by letting those governments know that you know what they are doing. The main way to do this is with a letter or telegram.

Do such protests do any good? Amnesty International says yes. "The letter and the telegram," says one Amnesty publication, "are remarkable for their power and simplicity. Sometimes a single letter is enough to improve a prisoner's situation. More often a government relents when it gets a sense that much of the world objects to its judgment."[3]

If you want to start writing letters on behalf of human rights on a regular basis, joining Amnesty International is probably the best way to do it (see next chapter). But it is not necessary to belong to Amnesty, or any other group, for you to write foreign officials on behalf of human rights. You can do so completely on your own. Tips for doing so will be found in Appendix B.

YOU HAVE CLOUT

Americans have a unique weapon to use in the battle for human rights: the enormous power and influence of the American government. Because of its position in the world, the U.S. can—when it wants to—exert tremendous influence on other countries. This is particularly true of the many countries whose governments depend on military and other help from the United States.

What is more, Americans have the clout that enables them to use this weapon. *Clout* means having influence with people who wield power, people who can get things done. Thanks to the system of representative democracy, Americans have clout with their politicians—including the president, senators, congresspersons, and the other elected officials who run the government.

Aryeh Neier of Human Rights Watch believes the single most important thing an ordinary person can do for the cause of human rights is to pressure the U.S. government to act on behalf of human rights.[4]

In order to use your clout, you have to let the politicians know what you think. All U.S. citizens have a right to do this, whatever their age or background. Some young people are reluctant to get in touch with elected officials. They assume that because they are too young to vote, no official will care what they think. But most of them do care.

Elected officials have to represent all their constituents. This means all the people in their district, regardless of their ages and voting habits. Besides, politicians know that the young person who was too young to vote in the last election is going to be old enough to vote in the next election, or the one after that.

It may seem strange, but some politicians are more interested in hearing from young people than they are from adults. As Robert Gifford, communications director for U.S. Senator Robert Kasten, explains, most adults have their political loyalties "pretty well set." If a politician is wise, he or she will try to earn the support of young constituents early, during their "formative political years."[5]

There are several ways to let elected officials know where you stand. According to Gifford, the three most common, and most effective, are writing the official a letter, speaking to one of his or her staff members, and speaking to the official in person.

Of the three, writing a letter is by far the most common. Letters to the president can be sent to the White House. Letters to senators or congresspersons either to their offices in Washington, D.C., or to the local offices most maintain in their home districts. While your letter will probably be read by a staff member, rather than by the president or the representatives themselves, your position will be on record. Added to the views of other constituents, it will be taken into account. Tips for writing letters to elected officials can be found in Appendix D.

Somewhat more effective, according to Gifford, is "bending the ear" of a member of the official's staff. If your senator or congressperson has a local office, you can simply make a phone call. Even better, stop by in person. Introduce yourself, explain what you are there for, and ask who you should talk to. In many cases, someone will be willing to talk to you right away. If the appropriate person is not there when you call, arrangements will be made for you to speak with him or her at some other time.

Talking to the official in person is the best alternative of all. But it is also the most difficult to arrange. Elected officials are incredibly busy. Lots of people want to talk to them every day. What is more, they have to travel a lot, and their plans are often subject to last minute changes. For all these reasons, it may be hard, or even impossible, to arrange a personal meeting. But you will not know until you try.

When you are asking for an appointment, it helps to have a specific reason for the meeting. If you want to persuade the official to vote a certain way on a bill, you might draw up a petition supporting this position. Once it is signed by a significant number of constituents (of whatever age), ask for the appointment to present the petition in person.

The best chance to obtain an appointment with a busy official is to "know someone who knows someone." If you know someone who knows the politician personally, or who was active in his or her campaign, they might be able to arrange an appointment for you. If not, write a very brief, thoughtful letter asking for an appointment. Follow it up with a phone call within a few days. Be flexible. If you are told that a meeting will be impossible within the next month, call back a month later and try again.

Whether you write, call, or speak to an elected official, the most important thing is that you have something to say. Know what you want to say before you write, call, or visit. Be prepared to state your position clearly—and briefly. Always be polite and respectful, in your tone as well as in your words. But do not be intimidated. Remember, what you have to say about human rights is important and deserves to be heard.

WHEN SHOULD YOU
USE YOUR CLOUT?

On what occasions should you attempt to contact a government official on behalf of human rights? The short answer is: on any occasion and no occasion at all. It is never out of place to impress your concern about human rights on your elected representatives. Senators, congresspersons and presidents have lots of things to think about. They are concerned with economic matters, with foreign policy, with the drug problem, with national defense, with all the thousands of details of government— and, of course, with getting reelected.

Most sides of important political issues have many lobbyists, people who try to persuade officials to vote their way on issues. Every representative is bombarded on every side by these lobbyists, pulling them this way and that way on every issue. It is easy for human rights to get lost in the turmoil.

The helpless victims of human rights abuses around the world have few lobbyists. You can be one. Your representatives need to know that constituents care about other things besides partisan politics and their own narrow economic interests. It is never out of place to remind our elected officials that we expect the American government to act in accordance with the principles laid down in the Constitution and the Universal Declaration of Human Rights.

In addition to expressing general concern about human rights matters, you can serve an important function by informing your representatives about these issues. Every representative has his or her areas of expertise—subjects and issues that are of special concern to them and that they know a lot about. Some senators and congresspersons are experts in the area of human rights, but most are not. Many know little more about the human rights situation in other countries than the average citizen does. You can help see that they get better informed by raising human rights issues and asking that they look into them. Ask them where they stand.

When legislation comes up that will have an impact on human rights matters, let your representatives know you care. Tell them that you believe the human rights consequences of the bill outweigh all other concerns. Always demand that the United States government take a strong, clear, and unconditional stand against human rights abuses everywhere in the world.

Occasionally, in your work for human rights, you may come across situations in which particular government officials might be of help. Do not hesitate to ask for that help. In late 1988, for example, I was talking to a member of a group that works for human rights in Latin America. He was concerned for the safety of a group of teachers in Colombia. A squad of terrorists had published their names on a "death list," and promised to kill them the next weekend. Appeals for protection to the Colombian government had produced no results. (This was probably because the teachers were outspoken opponents of the government.)

I knew that my own congressman, David Obey, was the chairman of a subcommittee that deals with economic aid to Latin America. I called the office he maintains in my hometown and explained the situation to his assistant. I expressed my fear for the safety of the teachers. His assistant said he would raise the issue with Congressman Obey.

The representative's office raised the issue with the U.S. State Department. Someone there raised the question with the department's people in Colombia. They determined that the teachers' situation was very dangerous and made sure that a representative from the U.S. embassy in Bogota made contact with the threatened teachers.[6]

Further word from Colombia has been hard to get. There is no way to tell whether the congressperson's intervention helped to save the lives of any of the teachers. But questions were raised in Washington and in Colombia. The Colombian government was made aware that people far away—people in the U.S. government—were concerned with the fate of a handful of dissident teachers in their country.

According to Aryeh Neier, "there is nothing more helpful to human rights around the world than this sort of process."[7] You or anyone else can participate in this process.

SEVEN

HOW TO JOIN A
HUMAN RIGHTS ORGANIZATION

Almost anything you can do alone, you can do even better working with others. First of all you can get more done. Two people can talk to twice as many people as one person can. They can make twice as many posters. They can pass out twice as many flyers. Three people can do even more.

Just as importantly, people working together can offer each other help and support. When one person's energy is low, another person can take up the slack. When one person's spirits are low, another person can often boost them up. In any kind of prolonged activity, there are bound to be disappointments. At those times, it helps to have people working together, to encourage each other and offer each other help.

There are several ways to find strength in numbers. One is simply to enlist friends to join you in your efforts. Another way is by joining an already existing human rights group.

Look around. Your own school or church may already have a club or other organization that deals with human rights issues. Hundreds of high schools and many more communities around the country have their own Amnesty International chapters. (Your regional office of Amnesty International U.S.A. can tell you about any chapters in your area.) Many churches have "social justice committees" or other organizations that work for human rights, whether in their own communities or in the world at large.

Keep in mind that not every group that works for human rights calls itself a human rights group. Many political, charitable, service, or even social organization have projects that relate to human rights. A church group that raises funds for the relief of refugees is doing something for human rights, even while it is carrying out the Biblical command to comfort the afflicted.

You may already belong to a group that could—with a little inspiration from you—get involved in human rights activities. If you belong to a club, scouting group, or other organization that undertakes projects, try to interest them in projects that promote human rights.

LET THE JOINER BEWARE

Before committing yourself to working with any human rights organization, you should find out everything you can about it. Different human rights groups have different interests and methods. Some focus on particular geographical regions, some on particular kinds of human rights. Some work largely within the United States, some work internationally.

Appendix E will give you the names, addresses, and major functions of several important human rights groups. There are many others. Choose one whose specific goals and methods have a special interest for you.

But beware. Just as some groups work for human rights without calling themselves human rights groups, some that claim to work for human rights are really working for something else. Be sure you understand what any group you join is trying to accomplish.

Take the case of a group that claims to work for human rights in Nicaragua. What does it mean by that? Both the Sandinista government of Nicaragua and the Contra rebels who oppose them have committed many serious human rights abuses. According to Amnesty International, the Sandinistas have taken literally thousands of political prisoners and held them for various lengths of time. Many of those who have been released complained of cruel treatment while they were in custody.[1] The Contras, on the other hand, have been guilty of murder and intimidation of peasants in the countryside. Their abuses have been so widespread, according to Laurence Birns, the director of the independent Council on Hemispheric Affairs, that the Contras failed to gain much support among the people of Nicaragua, even though they were fighting a very *un*popular government.[2]

So what does this particular group mean when it says it is supporting human rights in Nicaragua? Does it mean that it is supporting the Sandinistas in the hope that they will be able to crush the Contras? Or does it mean it is supporting the Contras in hope they will eventually overthrow the Sandinistas? Or does it really mean that it is working to end *all* the human rights abuses in Nicaragua, whichever side is committing them?

Once you are satisfied that the group is what it says it is, consider its methods. What does the group actually do? Does it spread the word about human rights within the United States? Monitor abuses abroad? Raise money to provide legal defenses for people accused of political crimes? Lobby the U.S. government? Write letters to foreign governments to free prisoners? Participate in demonstrations protesting abuses?

If the group holds meetings or participates in group activities, you may also want to take a look at its membership. Are these people you want to associate with? Would you be able to work well with them? Are you young, and most of them elderly? (Or vice versa?) Are you basically conservative, and all the others liberal—or even far to the left—in their political views? (Or vice versa?)

This is not to say that you should seek out a group in which everyone is just like you. You may, in fact, prefer to become involved with people very different from yourself. It might be said that the ideal human rights group is one that mirrors the differences within humanity itself—one that includes people of both sexes, and all ages, races, backgrounds, and political views.

It may be hard to get satisfactory answers to all these questions. You can be fairly sure that large, nationally respected organizations like those listed in Appendix E are legitimate. But with smaller, less-known organizations, your decision may boil down to a question of faith and trust. If you feel that you have not gotten satisfactory answers to all your questions, you should probably look around for another group to join. There are plenty of options open to anyone who wants to work for human rights.

CIVIL DISOBEDIENCE

One key question to ask about tactics is whether or not the group practices civil disobedience—deliberate illegal, but nonviolent acts.

There are many kinds of civil disobedience. Some church groups, for example, have offered sanctuary (protection) to illegal refugees from Central America. Although these refugees have fled war and political persecution in their own countries, U.S. immigration authorities have refused to accept them as immigrants. This means their presence in the United States is illegal. A few deeply concerned churches have taken some of these refugees in, refusing to cooperate with government efforts to send them back to the horrors in their own country.

By hiding the refugees, members of these groups sometimes break the law. They believe they are justified. For them, the safety of the refugees is more important than the immigration laws of the United States.

More typically, civil disobedience is committed as a way of drawing attention to a cause. Common attention-getting tactics include illegal demonstrations and sit-ins. (Sit-ins involve demonstrators who refuse to leave a public or private place when told

Two Salvadorean refugees participate in a
church service at the Immanuel Lutheran Church
in St. Louis. Many such political refugees
are considered illegal immigrants by the
U.S. government, prompting the formation of a
"sanctuary movement" among concerned churches.

to do so, in order to make a point. Civil rights demonstrators used this tactic a lot during the 1950s and '60s, e.g., sitting in at lunch counters that refused to serve black people and at other segregated facilities.)

These kinds of tactics can result in the arrest and jailing of demonstrators. In some cases, when police move in to break up an illegal demonstration or sit-in, demonstrators can be injured.

Before getting involved in any group that uses civil disobedience, you must ask yourself some very serious questions. Do you believe that such tactics are morally right? Are you willing to face physical danger, possible arrest, and even imprisonment for your cause?

FOUND AN AMNESTY INTERNATIONAL CHAPTER

If you are a high school or university student, you might want to start a chapter of Amnesty International U.S.A. at your school. Amnesty welcomes the participation of high school students. Unlike some adult groups, it knows what they can do.

As an Amnesty handbook written for students says: "The possibilities for human rights work in high schools are enormous. You have access to unique resources, such as school newspapers, classrooms, audiovisual equipment, teachers, and libraries. And *you* are the greatest resource of all. You can turn the chilling facts about human rights abuse into life-saving letters. You can stir up students and teachers and show them that they can make a difference for human rights."[3]

The procedure for starting an Amnesty chapter is a simple one. First you have to find a few other students who want to join too. They should be willing to write letters to free prisoners of conscience; to participate in publicity events and educational activities on behalf of human rights in your school and community; and to collect signatures on human rights petitions. You do not need a lot of people. Five or six eager members are enough to get started.

Then your group must find a faculty member willing to act as an adviser. This will not be hard in most cases. Many teachers care deeply about human rights. Having a faculty adviser can be helpful in many ways. He or she can help you with organizing, and in handling financial affairs. An adult adviser may also be useful in dealing with other adults in the community. If your group seeks support from community businesses or other outside organizations, it helps to have an adult who can be called to testify that you are legitimate.

More immediately, a sympathetic faculty member can help you get approval of your group from the school administration. Most schools have some process for gaining recognition as an official student organization or club. If yours is one of them, you should follow it.

Formal school recognition is not strictly required by Amnesty, but it can be vital to a school chapter's success. Recognition gives your group legitimacy in the eyes of students and faculty alike. In some schools it will enable you to use school facilities, and even school time, to carry out activities. For all these reasons John Mudore, the faculty adviser of an extremely successful Amnesty chapter at

Edgewood High School in Madison, Wisconsin, warns that "without the administration it won't get going."[4]

Once you and your friends have a faculty adviser, just write to your regional office of Amnesty International (see Appendix E). It will send you an AIUSA High School Group Sign-Up Form, which you simply fill out and return to them. The form requires you to designate one or two of your members as Amnesty International contact persons and asks for the name of your faculty adviser.

In return the regional office will put you in touch with an experienced Amnesty member to go to when you need help or advice. It will also begin sending you "Student Action," the newsletter for student chapters of Amnesty. Each month it will give you the case histories of prisoners of conscience in various countries together with the names and addresses of foreign officials to write to in their behalf.

You may also receive Urgent Action Appeals, which report crisis situations needing immediate intervention. The number of Appeals you get will vary, but there may be as many as four a month. Because you are a student group, they will usually involve victims who are either teachers, students, or other young people.

WHAT AMNESTY CHAPTERS DO

Your chapter will be asked to respond to the sufferings of these victims by writing letters in their support. And members don't have to stop at writing themselves. They can encourage others—

friends, other students, family members—to write too. These letters do not have to be long, and they take just moments to write. (See Appendix B for tips and samples.) But, added to the many similar letters written by members of other Amnesty chapters around the world, they can have remarkable effects.

The following testimony from a released prisoner in the Dominican Republic is dramatic evidence of what they can do.

> When the first two hundred letters came, the guards gave me back my clothes. Then the next two hundred letters came, and the prison director came to see me. When the next pile of letters arrived, the director got in touch with his superior. The letters kept coming and coming: three thousand of them. The President was informed. The letters still kept arriving, and the President called the prison and told them to let me go.[5]

Most chapters hold regular meetings, at which members meet to write letters, to share information and ideas, to hear guest speakers, watch videos on human rights, make plans for future activities, and—Amnesty strongly recommends—have some fun and refreshments. "Pizza," advises Amnesty, "is an ideal fuel for letter writing."[6]

School chapters carry out a variety of activities to help spread the word about human rights. They use all of the methods discussed in the previous chapter along with others that are made possible by their numbers and by the fact that they are an officially recognized school organization.

Different chapters around the country have

found all sorts of ways to get their message across. The Edgewood chapter in Madison, for example, sets up a table in the school cafeteria twice a month. Members staff the table, talking with other students about Amnesty and inviting them to write a letter or sign a petition to help free a prisoner. The table has proven to be an effective way not only of arousing interest in human rights, but of getting letters written as well.

Other chapters hand out flyers at school dances, school or local sporting events, and other places where people gather. (Before doing this, it is important to check the laws in your community. Some towns have laws that limit or forbid passing out printed materials in certain areas.) Amnesty members with a talent for public speaking offer themselves as speakers to other school, scouting, and community groups. They appear before them to talk to them about human rights issues and to encourage them to start Amnesty chapters of their own.

Some chapters hold parties to draw attention to human rights. This strategy can be enormously effective, as well as a lot of fun. On January 5, 1988, for example, twenty-three high school chapters in California and two in Cleveland, Ohio threw parties at the same time. All the parties were held in honor of the thirty-sixth birthday of a prisoner of conscience named Jiri Wolf. Wolf is a journalist and human rights activist who is serving a six-year sentence in a Czech prison. Ironically, his "crime" was writing about the Czechoslovakian prison system.

The parties got a lot of attention, and not just within the high schools. Two cities, Cleveland and

Palo Alto, California, joined in the spirit of the students' parties by officially declaring January 5th "Jiri Wolf Day."[7]

FINANCES

There are expenses involved in running any kind of organization. The expenses of a typical student Amnesty chapter are relatively small, but members must be prepared to meet them.

Every April each chapter has to make a report to Amnesty International U.S.A. (Amnesty will send you the form.) Besides serving as a financial record, this report lets the national organization know what your chapter has accomplished during the previous year.

Amnesty International U.S.A. requests a $50 annual fee from high school chapters. It does not insist on payment, however, if the group cannot afford it. In any case the first payment can be delayed until the group is firmly established. Future payments can be made at any time during the school year.[8]

Other expenses may include some money for stationery, as well as copying and printing costs for flyers and other informational materials. Postage for letters to foreign leaders is usually forty-five cents. Individual letter writers may want to contribute the cost of postage themselves, or the group can do it jointly. The total expense for a small student chapter may run as low as $80 or $100 a year, even including the $50 fee. A more typical chapter may need $150. An especially large or active chapter may need a bit more.

There are many ways to raise the money. Some

chapters get much of it from the school's student activity fund. This can be yet another advantage of being recognized as an official school organization. On the other hand, getting money from the school may bring unwelcome pressure from the school authorities along with it.

Some chapters sell Amnesty posters or T-shirts. Others hold Saturday car washes or monthly bake sales where they sell cookies, cakes, and pies contributed by sympathetic parents to the students.

Some chapters have shown remarkable imagination. Take the Egg-a-Thon conducted by the Edward R. Murrow High School in New York. Seven Amnesty members went door to door in their neighborhood. At the first door, a member would explain they were from Amnesty International and ask for the contribution of an egg. The member would take the egg next door and ask the person who answered if he would be willing to buy an egg from Amnesty International for any contribution he cared to give. In just three hours the seven students raised over one hundred dollars. This is enough to support many Amnesty chapters for an entire year.[9]

Fund-raising activities can be a lot of fun. Some chapters hold dances in their school gyms or organize school parties. Some sponsor concerts by local rock performers who follow the lead of such international stars as Sting and Tracy Chapman by donating their performance to the cause of human rights. The Watchung Hills High School in New Jersey raised a whopping nine hundred dollars from one concert.[10] If more money is raised than the chapter actually needs, the extra can always be sent on to Amnesty International.

Some Amnesty members enjoy fund-raising activities and have a knack for them. Others do not. Some experienced Amnesty advisers, like John Mudore, recommend going slow when it comes to fund-raising—particularly if a fund-raising event involves putting up a significant amount of money beforehand. "Remember," he cautions, "you can lose money too."[11]

In any case, fund-raising should always be combined with the more important purpose of spreading the word about human rights abuses. Human rights material should be prominently displayed and handed out, if possible, at all fund-raising events. When items are sold, discounts can be given to any customer who writes a letter on behalf of a prisoner of conscience. A letter was the price of admission to an Amnesty dance held at East Stroudsburg High School, in Pennsylvania. Dances and parties can always be used as occasions for writing letters or signing petitions. The Watchung rock concert didn't just raise a lot of money for Amnesty—it collected enough signatures to fill up twenty-five human rights petitions as well!

EIGHT

"MAKING THE WORLD A LITTLE LESS OPPRESSIVE, A LITTLE LESS HURTFUL"

It may be hard to understand, but human rights can be controversial. Americans who work for human rights within the United States do not face the kinds of physical risks faced by human rights campaigners in some other countries. But even here, taking a stand for human rights can be an unpopular thing to do.

Young people are sometimes surprised to be met with hostility when they talk about human rights. They find that many of their acquaintances, and even some of their friends, do not understand why they care. They regard taking a stand for any cause as a foolish—or even a peculiar—thing to do. They just "don't get it."

Some young people have been met with amusement—or even opposition—from their own parents when they became involved with human rights. The father of one deeply committed high school student named Miriam sometimes laughs at her concern for human rights. He thinks that she is foolish to imagine she can change the world. And besides, he argues, repression can be necessary—particularly when it might "save a country from the Communists."

"I'll argue for a while," Miriam says of her conversations with her father. But at a certain point "I have to stop." It is just too frustrating. But her father's scorn has not stopped her from working for human rights.[1]

BE PREPARED
FOR DISAPPOINTMENTS

Although many teachers and school administrators are extremely sympathetic to human rights in general, some are wary when their own students take a stand. This is particularly true when the students complain about human rights abuses committed by America's friends and allies around the world. They fear that the school might get involved in a public controversy. They worry that some parents might object.

Even an internationally respected organization like Amnesty International is suspect in some areas. Although hundreds of Amnesty chapters have been approved by high school administrations around the country, approval is not automatic.

Take the case of Francesca McCauslin, who tried to establish a chapter at her high school in Menomonie, Wisconsin, in 1987. Menomonie is a small town of less than thirteen thousand people in the western part of the state. It is, according to Francesca, a conservative community that is uncomfortable with change.

Still, she expected little trouble when she presented her plan for an Amnesty chapter to the school administration. A junior at Menomonie High, Francesca was already active in an Amnesty chapter at a nearby branch of the University of Wisconsin. She thought of Amnesty as a noncontroversial organization.

But when she brought her idea to the faculty member responsible for signing up new clubs, he turned it down flat. Amnesty International, he told her, was "too political." The school did not allow students to form "political" organizations.

Francesca was shocked. It hadn't occurred to her that anyone might think of Amnesty as "political." Looking the term up in the school's guidelines, she discovered that it meant "partisan": that is, favoring one political party over another. Amnesty, she knew, has always been strictly nonpartisan. But when she tried to explain this to school officials, they remained unmoved.

Together with several other students, many of whom were seniors, Francesca launched a campaign for her idea. The students received what she calls "quiet support" from several faculty members. The teachers told the students they approved. Some said they might be willing to serve as advisers to a school Amnesty chapter. But they didn't want their position made public until the administration gave its approval—if it ever did.

The students drew up a petition to take to the local school board, which had the power to overrule the administration's decision. The nine-member board had a reputation for being at least as timid as the administration itself, but it was the only hope the students had.

After much work officials ruled the petition invalid on a technicality, and the students had to start all over again. Finally, after six months of effort, the petition was ready. The board set a date to consider the matter. In the meantime the students sent letters to all the board members, explaining what Amnesty was all about.

When it came time for the vote, the board voted against them five to four. After all the time, and all their energy, and all the hope that they had put into it—the students had lost by a single vote!

On the face of it, the board's vote was a crushing defeat. And yet, in another way, Francesca thought, it was hopeful. Considering the conservative makeup of the board, Francesca felt the students received "wonderful support from some of the members." Even in the process of losing the final vote, the students had the satisfaction of knowing that they had educated several adults about the importance of human rights.

Francesca is trying again in her senior year. Whether or not she succeeds, her commitment to human rights will not end when she leaves Menomonie High. After graduation, she plans to go to Finland, to work with a Quaker peace project there. Ultimately, she hopes to continue working for human rights, either through Amnesty International or through the International Red Cross.

Even after her disappointments with the school administration and the school board, she is able to look back on her experience and conclude, "It's been very good for me."[2] It has also been good for the students and faculty at Menomonie High.

KEEPING A SENSE OF PERSPECTIVE

It is important that you—like Miriam and Francesca—keep a sense of perspective about your work for human rights. You are involved in a long-term struggle. Not everything you try to do will be immediately successful. Many of the people you try to persuade will not understand. Many—probably most—of the letters you write will not be answered. The repression, the torture, and the killing will continue in far too many places around the world. The fight against human rights abuses is a long and never-ending battle. It will not be won in a single skirmish. But it will not be lost in a single skirmish either.

As Bruce Springsteen said before embarking on the "Human Rights Now!" tour of benefit performances for Amnesty International in 1988: "It's not about changing the world overnight. It *is* about making the world . . . a little less oppressive, a little less hurtful."[3]

And that is something you do every time you work for human rights. Even when you seem to fail, you have taken another step in the process of educating others—and yourself—about the vital importance of human rights. Francesca McCauslin and her friends did not succeed in starting an Amnesty chapter at Menomonie High, but they persuaded four members of a hostile school board to vote with them and against the school administration. Francesca is trying again in her senior year. But even if she fails again, her campaign has inspired new allies. One of them, a sophomore, has promised that if the Amnesty chapter does not go through this year, he will carry on the fight for it next year.

Every time you talk to anyone about human rights, you are planting a seed. There is no telling when that seed will flower. Many have flowered already.

RECENT ADVANCES
IN HUMAN RIGHTS

The human rights situation today is much better than it used to be. The Nazi attempt at genocide against the Jews during World War II was not the last in this century. At least a million Buddhists were killed by the Khmer Rouge government of Kampuchea (Cambodia) during the 1970s. But genocide on that scale is no longer being practiced anywhere in the world. Forced labor still exists, but no country officially condones slavery. Legally enforced racial segregation, like the kind that existed in many American states until the 1960s, is all but a thing of the past. Only one country in the entire world—South Africa—legally withholds basic rights solely on the basis of a person's race.

The late 1980s, in particular, saw great increases in respect for human rights in an encouraging variety of countries. Some of the most dramatic changes occurred in the nations of Eastern Europe, which had long been among the worst abusers in the developed world. Under Mikhail Gorbachev, the Soviet Union led the way in making reforms that allow more political freedom than ever before.

But the Soviet Union was not alone. The government of the German Democratic Republic (East Germany), known as one of the most repressive in the world, released all its political prisoners and abolished the death penalty on July 17, 1987.[4] And in 1989 the Polish government relegalized the outlawed trade union Solidarity and even elected a Solidarity government.

New governments took over from repressive

regimes in countries from Pakistan to Paraguay, offering new hope for human rights in the 1990s. According to Secretary of State James Baker, even the Marxist government of war-torn Mozambique, one of the worst regimes in Africa, has moved "to more openness" in recent years.[5]

And as the 1980s came to an end, a promising new series of international human rights conferences was beginning. The last of them was scheduled to take place in Moscow—a location that would have been unthinkable for a human rights conference only a few years before.

But real advances in human rights are not brought about by governments. As an Amnesty International publication says,

> *The only real protection for human rights is people. People who speak out when they see human rights being violated. People who remind their governments, and all governments, that they won't sit still and let unjust imprisonment, torture and killings go on. People who demand that the international and domestic human rights standards be respected for every woman, man and child.*[6]

People like you.

APPENDIX A:
THE U.N. DECLARATION
OF HUMAN RIGHTS

On 10 December 1948, the General Assembly of the United Nations adopted and proclaimed the Universal Declaration of Human Rights, the full text of which appears in the following pages. Following this historic act, the Assembly called upon all Member countries to publicize the text of the Declaration and "to cause it to be disseminated, displayed, read and expounded principally in schools and other educational institutions, without distinction based on the political status of countries or territories."

Preamble

Whereas recognition of the inherent dignity and of the equal and inalienable rights of all members of the human family is the foundation of freedom, justice and peace in the world,

Whereas disregard and contempt for human rights have resulted in barbarous acts which have outraged the conscience of mankind, and the advent of a world in which human beings shall enjoy freedom of speech and belief and freedom from fear and want has been proclaimed as the highest aspiration of the common people,

Whereas it is essential, if man is not to be compelled to have recourse, as a last resort, to rebellion against tyranny and oppression, that human rights should be protected by the rule of law,

Whereas it is essential to promote the development of friendly relations between nations,

Whereas the peoples of the United Nations have in the Charter reaffirmed their faith in fundamental human rights, in the dignity and worth of the human person and in the equal rights of men and women and have determined to promote social progress and better standards of life in larger freedom,

Whereas Member States have pledged themselves to achieve, in co-operation with the UN, the promotion of universal respect for and observance of human rights and fundamental freedoms,

Whereas a common understanding of these rights and freedoms is of the greatest importance for the full realization of this pledge,

Now, therefore, The General Assembly *proclaims* this Universal Declaration of Human Rights as a common standard of achievement for all peoples and all nations, to the end that every individual and every organ of society, keeping this Declaration constantly in mind, shall strive by teaching and education to promote respect for these rights and freedoms and by progressive measures, national and international, to secure their universal and effective recognition and observance, both among the peoples of Member States themselves and among the peoples of territories under their jurisdiction.

Article 1

All human beings are born free and equal in dignity and rights. They are endowed with reason and conscience and should act towards one another in a spirit of brotherhood.

Article 2

Everyone is entitled to all the rights and freedoms set forth in this Declaration, without distinction of any kind, such as race, colour, sex, language, religion, political or other opinion, national or social origin, property, birth or other status.
Furthermore, no distinction shall be made on the basis of the political, jurisdictional or international status of the country or territory to which a person belongs, whether it be independent, trust, non–self-governing or under any other limitation of sovereignty.

Article 3

Everyone has the right to life, liberty and the security of person.

Article 4

No one shall be held in slavery or servitude; slavery and the slave trade shall be prohibited in all their forms.

Article 5

No one shall be subjected to torture or to cruel, inhuman or degrading treatment or punishment.

Article 6

Everyone has the right to recognition everywhere as a person before the law.

Article 7

All are equal before the law and are entitled without any discrimination to equal protection of the law. All are entitled to equal protection against any discrimination in violation of this Declaration and against any incitement to such discrimination.

Article 8

Everyone has the right to an effective remedy by the competent national tribunals for acts violating the fundamental rights granted him by the constitution or by law.

Article 9

No one shall be subjected to arbitrary arrest, detention or exile.

Article 10

Everyone is entitled in full equality to a fair and public hearing by an independent and impartial tribunal, in the determination of his rights and obligations and of any criminal charge against him.

Article 11

1. Everyone charged with a penal offense has the right to be presumed innocent until proved guilty according to law in a public trial at which he has had all the guarantees necessary for his defense.

2. No one shall be held guilty of any penal offense on account of any act or omission which did not constitute a penal offense, under national or international law, at the time when it was committed. Nor shall a heavier penalty be imposed than the one that was applicable at the time the penal offense was committed.

Article 12

No one shall be subjected to arbitrary interference with his privacy, family, home or correspondence, nor to attacks upon his honour and reputation. Everyone has the right to the protection of the law against such interference or attacks.

Article 13

1. Everyone has the right to freedom of movement and residence within the borders of each State.

2. Everyone has the right to leave any country, including his own, and to return to his country.

Article 14

1. Everyone has the right to seek and to enjoy in other countries asylum from persecution.

2. This right may not be invoked in the case of prosecutions genuinely arising from non-political crimes or from acts contrary to the purposes and principles of the United Nations.

Article 15

1. Everyone has the right to a nationality.

2. No one shall be arbitrarily deprived of his nationality nor denied the right to change his nationality.

Article 16

1. Men and women of full age, without any limitation due to race, nationality or religion, have the right to marry and to found a family. They are entitled to equal rights as to marriage, during marriage and at its dissolution.

2. Marriage shall be entered into only with the free and full consent of the intending spouses.

3. The family is the natural and fundamental group unit of society and is entitled to protection by society and the State.

Article 17

1. Everyone has the right to own property alone as well as in association with others.

2. No one shall be arbitrarily deprived of his property.

Article 18

Everyone has the right to freedom of thought, conscience and religion; this right includes freedom to change his religion or belief, and freedom, either alone or in community with others and in public or private, to manifest his religion or belief in teaching, practice, worship and observance.

Article 19

Everyone has the right to freedom of opinion and expression; this right includes freedom to hold opinions without interference and to seek, receive and impart information and ideas through any media and regardless of frontiers.

Article 20

1. Everyone has the right to freedom of peaceful assembly and association.

2. No one may be compelled to belong to an association.

Article 21

1. Everyone has the right to take part in the government of his country, directly or through freely chosen representatives.

2. Everyone has the right of equal access to public service in his country.

3. The will of the people shall be the basis of the authority of government; this will shall be expressed in periodic and genuine elections which shall be by universal and equal suffrage and shall be held by secret vote or by equivalent free voting procedures.

Article 22

Everyone, as a member of society, has the right to social security and is entitled to realization, through national effort and international co-operation and in accordance with the organization and resources of each State, of the economic, social and cultural rights indispensable for his dignity and the free development of his personality.

Article 23

1. Everyone has the right to work, to free choice of employment, to just and favourable conditions of work and to protection against unemployment.

2. Everyone, without any discrimination, has the right to equal pay for equal work.

3. Everyone who works has the right to just and favourable remuneration ensuring for himself and his family an existence worthy of human dignity, and supplemented, if necessary, by other means of social protection.

4. Everyone has the right to form and to join trade unions for the protection of his interests.

Article 24

Everyone has the right to rest and leisure, including reasonable limitation of working hours and periodic holidays with pay.

Article 25

1. Everyone has the right to a standard of living adequate for the health and well-being of himself and of his family, including food, clothing, housing and medical care and necessary social services, and the right to security in the event of unemployment, sickness, disability, widowhood, old age or other lack of livelihood in circumstances beyond his control.

2. Motherhood and childhood are entitled to special care and assistance. All children, whether born in or out of wedlock, shall enjoy the same social protection.

Article 26

1. Everyone has the right to education. Education shall be free, at least in the elementary and fundamental stages. Elementary education shall be compulsory. Technical and professional education shall be made generally available and higher education shall be equally accessible to all on the basis of merit.

2. Education shall be directed to the full development of the human personality and to the strengthening of respect for human rights and fundamental freedoms. It shall promote understanding, tolerance and friendship among all nations, racial or religious groups, and shall further the activities of the United Nations for the maintenance of peace.

3. Parents have a prior right to choose the kind of education that shall be given to their children.

Article 27

1. Everyone has the right freely to participate in the cultural life of the community, to enjoy the arts and to share in scientific advancement and its benefits.

2. Everyone has the right to the protection of the moral and material interests resulting from any scientific, literary or artistic production of which he is the author.

Article 28

Everyone is entitled to a social and international order in which the rights and freedoms set forth in this Declaration can be fully realized.

Article 29

1. Everyone has duties to the community in which alone the free and full development of his personality is possible.

2. In the exercise of his rights and freedoms, everyone shall be subject only to such limitations as are determined by law solely for the purpose of securing due recognition and respect for the rights and freedoms of others and of meeting the just requirements of morality, public order and the general welfare in a democratic society.

3. These rights and freedoms may in no case be exercised contrary to the purposes and principles of the United Nations.

Article 30

Nothing in this Declaration may be interpreted as implying for any State, group or person any right to engage in any activity or to perform any act aimed at the destruction of any of the rights and freedoms set forth herein.

APPENDIX B:
TIPS ON WRITING LETTERS
TO FOREIGN GOVERNMENTS

According to Amnesty International, "Letters may be handwritten or typed. The most important thing about letter writing is to be careful that the letters express your concern about the situation of imprisonment, torture, or human rights abuse, and be written in a respectful, polite manner."

1. Whenever possible address the letter to a specific official or dignitary. This might be the president, prime minister or other head of the government involved, or some lesser official. The name of most countries' heads of government can be found in either *The World Almanac* (New York: World Almanac) or the *Statesmen's Year Book* (New York: St. Martin's Press). Mailing addresses for such officials can often be found in *The International Who's Who*. If all else fails, send your letter to the country's ambassador to the United States, in care of that country's embassy in Washington, D.C. Embassy addresses are in the Washington, D.C. phone book, available at most libraries.

2. Be neat. Unless your handwriting is exceptionally good, it is best to type your letter. But always sign in ink, and in longhand.

3. Unless you are fluent in the language of the country you are writing to, write in English.

4. Keep your letter short and to the point. Express your concern over the situation you are writing about and make a clear request that something be done to correct it.

5. Be specific. A letter to a foreign government does not have to be well written. Foreign officials do not care about your literary style. But it does have to be clear. Use names, dates, and other facts whenever possible. When dealing with cases of specific prisoners, it is vital to make clear exactly who you are talking about, and what it is you are objecting to.

6. Regardless of how enraged you feel, be polite. Amnesty recommends that you avoid making direct accusations. "It is better to assume that the authorities are either not informed or are willing to seek a remedy to alleged violations of human rights." Always remember, you cannot force a government to be fair or just. You are making a request, not issuing an order. You want to influence the government to act decently, not to anger it.

7. Don't argue politics. Remember, you are writing on behalf of human rights, which are above politics. Besides, you are not going to change the government's ideology.

8. It can be useful to mention an article of the Universal Declaration of Human Rights, or some other international agreement the country has signed, in support of your request.

9. Sign your letter with a formal complimentary close, such as "Respectfully yours," or "Sincerely yours."

The following are samples of typical letters, provided by Amnesty International U.S.A.

Your Excellency,

I appeal for the release of ——— ———, a prisoner of conscience who has been held in Ngaragba Prison for the last three years. I urge you to take a personal interest in this case and ensure that [he or she] is allowed to rejoin [his or her] family.

Yours truly,
(Signature)

Dear Prime Minister,

I am a teacher ... I am concerned about the plight of ——— ———, who has been detained for nearly three years under the Internal Security Act. No reason has been given for her detention.

Her imprisonment violates Article 9 of the Universal Declaration of Human Rights, which states: "No one shall be subjected to arbitrary arrest, detention, or exile." I therefore urge you to look into this case urgently and to order the release of ——— ———.

Yours sincerely,
(Signature)

Your Excellency,

I am writing to ask for the immediate and unconditional release of ————— —————, who I believe has been imprisoned for the nonviolent exercise of [his or her] right to freedom of expression in violation of the Universal Declaration of Human Rights.

Yours sincerely,
(Signature)

APPENDIX C:
TIPS ON WRITING
A LETTER TO THE EDITOR

1. Keep your letter short. Most newspapers have a strict maximum length for letters. The requirement varies from paper to paper. Sometimes it will be stated in the letters column of the paper itself. If not, call the paper's office and find out.

2. Whenever possible, frame your letter so that it responds to some story or editorial printed in a recent issue of the paper. This will greatly improve the chance of your letter being published. This is particularly vital when writing to a large newspaper or magazine that has to choose from among many letters competing for space. If your letter disagrees with the earlier feature, state clearly the position or misinformation you are objecting to, and explain your objection. If your letter is in support of an earlier article, thank the editor for publishing it, then add your own comments as clearly and as briefly as you can.

3. Be specific. A letter to the editor is more like a poster than an essay. You should limit yourself to one main point in every letter. Several facts can be mentioned to support your position, but the central point should be stated as simply and clearly as possible.

4. The more well-written your letter, the more likely it will be published, and the more convincing it will be when it is read. This means you should not sit down, write your letter, and send it off in a rush of inspiration. Even professional writers have to rewrite their copy, often several times, to make it effective. So should you.

APPENDIX D:
TIPS ON WRITING LETTERS
TO ELECTED OFFICIALS

Many of the same rules that apply to letters written for publication apply to letters to elected officials as well. They include the need to be neat, brief, polite, clear, and to the point.

In addition there are some special considerations when writing to an elected representative. They include the following:

1. If you are a constituent of the representative to whom you are writing, be sure to say so.

2. If you are writing on behalf of a group of any kind, say that too. If the group has its own stationery, use its letterhead to write your letter.

3. If you have ever voted for, or worked for, the politician in the past, it never hurts to point that out as well.

4. Explain briefly why the issue is important to you.

5. Give the representative a reason to care about the issue. Point out how it relates to a particular responsibility or interest of his or her own. When you are writing in support or opposition to a specific bill, that relationship may be obvious. If it is not, find one. For example, if you are concerned about the atrocities being committed by death squads in El Salvador and your congressperson or senator sits on a committee that deals with requests for military aid to El Salvador, point this out. Ask him or her to vote against aid to a government that allows such death squads to operate. Or point out that a human rights worker from the congressperson's own district is in danger from the death squads. (In

order to find out what committees your congressperson and senator sits on, simply call up their offices and ask.)

6. Do not just tell a representative where you stand on an issue, ask where he or she stands as well. Most politicians answer their mail or have it answered by staff members. At the very least, your question will force staff members to find out what position their boss takes on the issue. If the representative has not already taken a position, your question may force her or him to do so.

Correspondence to U.S. senators and congresspersons can be addressed as follows:

To United States Senators:
    Senator (Name)
    c/o U.S. Senate
    Washington, D.C. 20510

To United States Congresspersons:
    The Honorable (Name)
    c/o U.S. House of Representatives
    Washington, D.C. 20515

In addition, most senators and congresspersons operate at least one office in their local district. Check under the representative's name in your local phone book to see if there is one in your community.

APPENDIX E:
SOME LEADING HUMAN
RIGHTS ORGANIZATIONS

The following are just a few of the hundreds of human rights organizations active in the United States.

American Association for the
  International Commission of Jurists
777 United Nations Plaza
New York, NY 10017

Works with United Nations organizations to promote human rights and to establish better procedures for protecting them around the world.

American Christians for the Abolition of Torture
300 W. Apsley Street
Philadelphia, PA 19144

Works from a Christian perspective to eliminate torture.

American Civil Liberties Union
122 Maryland Ave., N.E.
Washington, DC 20002

Fights to protect and expand civil and political rights within the United States.

American Friends Service Committee
1501 Cherry Street
Philadelphia, PA 19102

Works to end human rights abuses and to give assistance to individual victims of torture.

Amnesty International U.S.A. (Regional Headquarters)

Works to eliminate torture and the death penalty and to free "prisoners of conscience" everywhere.

Mid-Atlantic Region (Includes Delaware, District of Columbia, Maryland, Pennsylvania, Virginia, and West Virginia.)

608 Massachusetts Ave., N.E.
Washington, DC 20002

Southern Region (Includes Alabama, Arkansas, Florida, Georgia, Louisiana, Mississippi, North Carolina, Oklahoma, South Carolina, Tennessee, and Texas.)

730 Peachtree, Room 982
Atlanta, GA 30308

Midwestern Region (Includes Illinois, Indiana, Iowa, Kansas, Kentucky, Michigan, Minnesota, Missouri, Nebraska, North Dakota, Ohio, South Dakota, and Wisconsin.)

53 W. Jackson, Room 1162
Chicago, IL 60604

Western Region (Includes Alaska, Arizona, California, Colorado, Hawaii, Idaho, Montana, Nevada, New Mexico, Oregon, Utah, Washington, and Wyoming.)

3407 W. 6th Street #704
Los Angeles, CA 90020

655 Sutter Street #402
San Francisco, CA 94102

New England Region (Includes Connecticut, Maine, Massachusetts, New Hampshire, New Jersey, New York, Rhode Island, and Vermont.)

58 Day Street/Davis Square
Somerville, MA 02144

Fund for Free Expression
485 Fifth Ave., 3rd Floor
New York, NY 10036

Affiliated with Human Rights Watch (see listing below), this organization promotes free speech by combatting censorship around the world.

Human Rights Watch
485 Fifth Avenue, 3rd Floor
New York, NY 10017

This is an umbrella organization that monitors and reports on human rights abuses around the world and tries to influence U.S. foreign policy to help end them. It includes

1. Americas Watch. Researches and focuses public attention on human rights violations in Latin America

2. Helsinki Watch. Concentrates on abuses in Turkey and the countries of the Soviet bloc

3. Asia Watch. Monitors human rights abuses in the countries of Asia and the Far East

4. Africa Watch. A new branch that began operations in 1988.

5. Middle East Watch. Scheduled to begin operations in 1989

International League for Human Rights
432 Park Avenue South
New York, NY 10016

Helps victims of torture and researches and publishes reports about human rights violations around the world.

National Headquarters of the American Red Cross
17th and D Streets, N.W.
Washington, DC 20006

United States branch of the International Red Cross, whose International Committee helps refugees from war and other disasters, promotes laws that outlaw torture, and protects prisoners of war and civilians caught up in war situations.

Physicians for Human Rights
58 Day St.
Suite 202
Somerville, MA 02144

Works to investigate and document medical aspects of human rights abuses.

World Council of Churches (U.S. Conference)
475 Riverside Drive, Room 1062
New York, NY 10115

An organization of Protestant and Orthodox churches working to aid refugees and to combat racism as well as to focus the attention of its member churches on human rights, including the right to dissent, the freedom from political suppression, and the abolition of torture.

SOURCE NOTES

Chapter One

1. For more information about Stephen Biko and his struggle against apartheid, see *Biko* by Donald Woods (New York: Paddington Press, 1978).
2. Marci McDonald, "The Global Struggle for Human Rights," *Macleans*, November 24, 1980.
3. Milton Meltzer, *The Human Rights Book* (New York: Farrar, Straus & Giroux, 1979), 87.
4. Statement of U.S. Assistant Secretary of State for Human Rights and Humanitarian Affairs, Richard Schifter, before Congress, on May 6, 1987. Published in the *Department of State Bulletin* (August 1987), 78.
5. *Human Rights Watch* (periodical) (October–November 1988), 11.
6. *Amnesty International Report 1988*. (London: Amnesty International, 1988), 131.
7. Ibid., 119.
8. "A History of Dedication to the Cause of Human Rights," *U.N. Chronicle* (March 1988), 50.
9. In the Foreword to *International Human Rights, Society, and the Schools* (Washington, D.C.: National Council for the Social Studies, 1982), ix.
10. For the complete text of *The Universal Declaration of Human Rights* see Appendix A.

11. This, together with many other insights into some young people's commitment to human rights, was gained from a long conversation between the author and Karen Danner, Jessica Foeste, Melissa O'Loughlin, Steve Barmette, Eva Schulte, Rachel Berthold, Miriam Willmann, and Anne O'Brien—eight bright and committed members of the Amnesty International chapter at Edgewood High School, in Madison, Wisconsin, on December 21, 1988.
12. Quoted by Robert F. Drinan, S.J., in "Religion and the Future of Human Rights," *The Christian Century*, August 12–19, 1987, 687.
13. *Department of State Bulletin* (February 1985), 21.
14. "Human Rights Day Proclamation, 1980," reprinted in the *Department of State Bulletin* (February 1981), 54.

Chapter Two

1. This covenant, along with several other key human rights documents, can be found in *The Human Rights Book*.
2. Jacques Maritain, *The Rights of Man* (London: 1944), 37.
3. Robert F. Drinan, S.J., "Religion and the Future of Human Rights," *The Christian Century*, August 12–19, 1987, 683.
4. Quoted in *Birthright of Man* (New York: UNIPUB, 1969), 555. This valuable selection of texts and quotations related to human rights was prepared under the direction of Jeanne Hersch and published by the United Nations.
5. Quoted in *Birthright*, 175.
6. From *The Way of Kings*, as quoted in *Birthright*, 522.
7. From *Hadith* (*The Sayings of the Prophet*), as quoted in *Birthright*, 508.
8. Quoted in *Birthright*, 22.
9. For a more detailed discussion of the Age of Enlightenment and its effects on modern political thinking, see Michael Kronenwetter's *Are You a Liberal? Are You a Conservative?* (New York: Watts, 1984).
10. For a discussion of freedom of the press in American history, see Michael Kronenwetter's *Politics and the Press* (New York: Watts, 1987).
11. "People Only Live Full Lives in the Light of Human Rights," *U.N. Chronicle* (March 1988), 4.
12. The charter of the United Nations. Reprints of the charter are available from many sources, including the U.N. itself. Excerpts appear in Meltzer, beginning on page 164.

13. Ibid., 167.
14. Quoted in the *U.N. Chronicle* (March 1988), 46.
15. Quoted in "Building Moral Outrage," *Time,* October 17, 1988, 22.
16. *Amnesty International Report 1988,* 15.
17. Ibid., 277.
18. Robert F. Drinan, S.J., "Religion and the Future of Human Rights," *The Christian Century,* 685.

Chapter Three

1. Ira Glasser, National Executive Director of the ACLU, speaking before the National Press Club, Washington, D.C., on October 6, 1988, and broadcast over C-SPAN cable television network.
2. See *The Persecution of Human Rights Monitors, December 1987 to December 1988* (New York: Human Rights Watch, 1988), 5.
3. *Amnesty International Report 1988,* 235.
4. *Introduction to Amnesty International,* 5.
5. Vita Bite, "Human Rights in U.S. Foreign Relations: Six Key Questions in the Continuing Foreign Policy Debate," Congressional Research Service Report No. 81–257 F, Washington, D.C., 1981, 6–7.
6. "The Common Sense of Human Rights," first printed in *The Wall St. Journal,* April 8, 1981, and reprinted in Thomas Draper's *Human Rights* (New York: H. W. Wilson Company, 1982), 123.
7. For a fuller discussion of both Carter's and Reagan's human rights positions, and of the whole issue of human rights and U.S. foreign policy, see Stephen Goode's *The Foreign Policy Debate: Human Rights and American Foreign Policy* (New York: Watts, 1984).
8. Warren Christopher, "Human Rights and the National Interest," in a speech before the American Bar Association, August 4, 1980. Reprinted in *Human Rights* edited by Thomas Draper.
9. Quoted in Goode, 48.
10. This is the United Nations' definition, as simplified in "Introduction to Amnesty International," an undated publication of Amnesty International U.S.A., edited by Nina Feldman, 6.
11. *Torture by Governments* (Amnesty International, U.S.A., 1984), 36.

12. Interviewed by Philipe Nobile in the *San Francisco Chronicle* and quoted in *Torture by Governments,* 37.
13. Quoted in *The Human Rights Book,* 92.
14. Ibid.

Chapter Four

1. This chapter relies largely on two sources for its assessment of the human rights situation in various countries of the world. They are the *Amnesty International Report 1988* (London: Amnesty International Publications, 1988), and Charles Humana's *World Human Rights Guide* (New York: Pica Press, 1983). For the most part, notes will be used for information from these sources only when individual cases or specific statistics are cited.
2. Brenda M. Branaman, *South Africa: Recent Developments* (A Congressional Research Service Issue Brief, 1988), 7.
3. Humana, 124.
4. Ibid., 214.
5. *Amnesty International Report 1988,* 239.
6. *Amnesty Action* (March/April 1988), 3.
7. *Amnesty International Report 1988,* 181.
8. Ivo D. Duchacek, *Rights and Liberties in the World Today: Constitutional Promise and Reality* (Santa Barbara: Clio Press, 1973), 70.
9. Humana, 48.
10. *Amnesty International Report 1988,* 112.
11. Ibid., 103.
12. Ibid., 125.
13. Ibid., 215
14. Humana, 224.
15. Monitor Radio news reports, December 1, 1988.
16. *Torture by Governments,* 41.
17. *Amnesty International Report 1988,* 14.
18. Ibid, 273–77.
19. Ibid.

Chapter Five

1. For a biography of Elizabeth Cady Stanton, see *In Her Own Right: the Life of Elizabeth Cady Stanton* by Elizabeth Griffith (New York: Oxford University Press, 1984).
2. For a more detailed account of Gandhi's life and work, see

Louis Fischer's *The Life of Mahatma Gandhi* (New York: Macmillan, 1962).

3. There are many books dealing with Dr. Martin Luther King, Jr., and the civil rights movement. Among the best and most recent are David J. Garrow's *Bearing the Cross: Martin Luther King, Jr. and the Southern Christian Leadership Conference* (New York: William Morrow and Company, Inc., 1986) and Taylor Branch's *Parting the Waters: America in the King Years, 1954–1963* (New York: Simon & Schuster, 1988).

4. See Walesa's autobiography, *A Way of Hope* (New York: H. Holt & Co., 1987).

5. Brenda M. Branaman, *South Africa: Recent Developments* (A Congressional Research Service Issue Brief, 1988), 5.

6. The Nobel Peace Prize citation, quoted in the article on Archbishop Tutu in *Funk & Wagnalls New Encyclopedia* (Ramsey, N.J.: Funk & Wagnalls, 1986), volume 26, 125.

7. Aryeh Neier, in the Introduction to *The Persecution of Human Rights Monitors* (New York: Human Rights Watch, 1988), 7.

8. Ibid., 1.

9. Ibid., 1–2.

10. *Introduction to Amnesty International*, 3.

11. "Human Rights," *Time*, October 17, 1988, 22.

12. *Amnesty International Report 1988*, 278.

13. An appeal for letters in support of El-Bou went out in the September 1988 *Student Action* (Amnesty International Northeast College Newsletter edition), 10.

14. *Amnesty International U.S.A. An Introduction*, an undated publication of Amnesty International U.S.A., 1.

15. "Good News From Norway," *The Christian Century*, October 26, 1977, 973.

16. Martin Ennals, then the secretary-general of Amnesty International, quoted in "The World's Conscience," *Newsweek*, October 24, 1977, 61.

17. Quoted in *Amnesty International U.S.A. An Introduction*, 10.

Chapter Six

1. Speech before the National Press Club in Washington, D.C., November 6, 1988, telecast over the C-SPAN cable television network.

2. *Argentina: the Military Juntas and Human Rights* (London: Amnesty International, 1988).

3. *Amnesty International U.S.A. An Introduction*, 8.

4. Interviewed on Wisconsin Public Radio, December 22, 1988.
5. Interview with author.
6. Conversation between the author and Jerry Madison, of Rep. David Obey's staff.
7. Wisconsin Public Radio interview.

Chapter Seven

1. *Amnesty International Report 1988*, 125.
2. Interview on C-SPAN television, January 24, 1989.
3. *Working for Amnesty International in Your High School*, an uncopyrighted publication of Amnesty International U.S.A., 1.
4. Interviewed by the author, October 26, 1988.
5. Quoted in *Amnesty International U.S.A. An Introduction*, 4.
6. *Working for Amnesty . . .* , 13.
7. *Amnesty Action* (March/April 1988), 5.
8. *Working for Amnesty . . .* , 17.
9. *High School Meeting and Events Handbook*, an uncopyrighted publication of Amnesty International U.S.A., 7.
10. Ibid.

Chapter Eight

1. Conversation with Edgewood High School students, December 22, 1988.
2. This account of Francesca McCauslin's experience at Menomonie High is based on lengthy phone interviews with Francesca herself and with Ed Gold, of the University of Wisconsin/Stout chapter of Amnesty International, Menomonie, Wisconsin.
3. A National Public Radio interview, September 20, 1988, prior to the 1988 *Human Rights Now!* tour.
4. *Amnesty International Report 1988*, 201.
5. Testimony of Secretary of State designee James Baker at his confirmation hearings before the U.S. Senate Foreign Relations Committee, January 17, 1989.
6. *Working for Amnesty International in Your High School*, 6.

FOR FURTHER READING

Books

Alderson, George, and Sentman, Everett. *How You Can Influence Congress: The Complete Handbook for the Citizen Lobbyist.* (New York: E.P. Dutton, 1979).

Amnesty International Report 1989 (London: Amnesty International Publications, 1989). The latest edition of Amnesty International's annual country-by-country report on the state of human rights.

Birthright of Man (New York: UNIPUB, 1969). A selection of quotations and texts, relating to human rights, prepared under the direction of Jeanne Hersch.

Chalidze, Valery. *To Defend These Rights: Human Rights and the Soviet Union,* translated by Guy Daniels. (New York: Random House, 1974).

Draper, Thomas, ed. *Human Rights* (New York: H.W. Wilson, 1982). A collection of significant speeches and articles from several sources and points of view.

Duchacek, Ivo D. *Rights and Liberties in the World Today: Constitutional Promise and Reality* (Santa Barbara: Clio Press, 1973). A study comparing the constitutional bills of rights of various countries, to each other and to the actual state of human rights in those countries as of the time the book was written.

Goode, Stephen. *The Foreign Policy Debate—Human Rights and American Foreign Policy* (New York: Watts, 1984). An objective look at the continuing debate over the role human rights should play in American foreign policy.

Human Rights Guide. Compiled by *The Economist.* (New York: Facts on File, 1984). An attempt to rate most of the countries of the world according to their respect—or lack of it—for human rights.

Laqueur, Walter, and Rubin, Barry. *The Human Rights Reader* (Philadelphia: Temple University Press, 1979).

Meltzer, Milton. *The Human Rights Book* (New York: Farrar, Straus & Giroux, 1979).

Reports, Magazine Articles and Other Publications

The Persecution of Human Rights Monitors, December 1987 to December 1988. (New York: Human Rights Watch, 1988).

Torture by Governments. A Seven Part Educational Guide for High Schools. (Amnesty International U.S.A., 1984).

"A History of Dedication." *U.N. Chronicle* (March 1988), 45.

Amnesty Action. A regular newsletter, published for members of Amnesty International U.S.A., New York.

Bite, Vita. "Human Rights in U.S. Foreign Relations: Six Key Questions in the Continuing Policy Debate." A report of the Congressional Research Service of the Library of Congress, Washington, D.C., 1981.

Branson, Margaret Stimmann, and Torney-Purta, Judith, eds. *International Human Rights, Society, and the Schools.* National Council for the Social Studies Bulletin, no. 68. (Washington, D.C.: National Council for the Social Studies, 1982).

"Human Rights Watch," *Newsletter,* published by Human Rights Watch, and the Fund for Free Expression, New York City. Annual subscription $15.

Lister, George. "U.S. Human Rights Policy: Origins and Implementation," *Department of State Bulletin* (August 1987), 73.

Reagan, Ronald. "Rededication to the Cause of Human Rights," *Department of State Bulletin* (February 1985), 21.

Schifter, Richard. "The Human Rights Issue in Korea," *Department of State Bulletin* (August 1987), 77.

Both Amnesty International U.S.A. and Human Rights Watch publish several reports each year on specific human rights issues. For a bibliography of these reports, as well as information on how to order them, contact the organization concerned.

INDEX

Soh Joon Shik, 14, 16
Solidarity trade union, 75, 122
Somalia, 16–17
Somoza, Anastasio, 49, 50
South Africa, 11, 13, 41, 55–56, 60, *62*, 63–64, 73, 75, 84–85, 92
Soviet Union, 14, 41, 55, 56, 59, 69, 77, 122
Spain, 57, 69
Springsteen, Bruce, 89, 121
Sri Lanka, 55, 60
Stalin, Joseph, 41
Stanton, Elizabeth Cady, 71–72
State Department, U.S., 102
Sting, 91
Stone, Lucy, 72

Taiwan, 57
Tamils, 60
Torture, 37, 50–53, 68–69
Totalitarian states, 56
Tunisia, 69
Turkey, 67
Tutu, Desmond, 73, *74*, 75

Uganda, 41, 69
U.N. Convention against Torture, 68–69
U.N. Convention on Prevention of Genocide, 36
United Nations, 34, *35*, 36–39, 68–69, 124

United States:
   foreign policy, 47, 49–50
   founding of, 28–31
   human rights abuses, 31, 42–43, 59, 71–72
   monitoring human rights in, 79
   as symbol of human rights, 21–22
   U.N. documents, failure to sign, 38–39
Universal Declaration of Human Rights, 18, 21, *35*
   importance of, 37–38
   rights protected by, 36–37
   text of, 124–31
Urgent Action Appeals, 111
U2, 89

Vance, Cyrus, 50
Volel, Yves, 17–18

Walesa, Lech, 75–76
Wars and revolutions, 20–21
Wolf, Jiri, 113
Women, discrimination against, 57, *58*, 59, 71–72
World Council of Churches, 141
World Human Rights Guide, 64
World War II, 34, 36

Zambia, 55

ABOUT
THE AUTHOR

Michael Kronenwetter is a free-lance writer who has been a newspaper columnist and media critic. He has also had a radio play produced by Wisconsin Public Radio. His other books for Franklin Watts include *Free Press v. Fair Trial, Are You a Liberal? Are You a Conservative?*, *The Threat from Within: Unethical Politics and Politicians,* and *The Military Power of the President.* He lives with his family in Wausau, Wisconsin.